Safe House

James Heneghan

ORCA BOOK PUBLISHERS

Library and Archives Canada Cataloguing in Publication

Heneghan, James, 1930-
Safe house / James Heneghan.

ISBN 1-55143-640-X

I. Title.

PS8565.E581S23 2006   jC813'.54   C2006-903100-2

Summary: Liam is orphaned and alone, on the run from vicious killers.

First published in the United States, 2006
Library of Congress Control Number: 2006927982

Orca Book Publishers gratefully acknowledges the support for its publishing
programs provided by the following agencies: the Government of Canada
through the Book Publishing Industry Development Program and the
Canada Council for the Arts, and the Province of British Columbia through
the BC Arts Council and the Book Publishing Tax Credit.

Cover design: Lynn O'Rourke
Cover photography: Every effort was made to
determine the rights holder of the cover image.

Orca Book Publishers   Orca Book Publishers
Box 5626, Stn. B   PO Box 468
Victoria, BC Canada   Custer, WA USA
V8R 6S4   98240-0468

www.orcabook.com
Printed and bound in Canada

09 08 07 06 • 4 3 2 1

For my children.

My grateful thanks to Lucy Scott and Norma Charles for reading the manuscript and offering suggestions on matters literary, to Olive John and Neil Savage for their expertise on matters Irish, and to my patient and perceptive editor Andrew Wooldridge for all his hard work.

Will you come to our wee party, will you come?

Bring your own ammunition and a gun,

For Catholics and Protestants will be there, blowing each other in the air.

Will you come to our wee party, will you come?

Belfast streetsong, circa 1935

from *Keep the Kettle Boiling* by Maggi Kerr Peirce

The Appletree Press, Belfast, N.I., 1983

...masked men with guns...

It was the perfect night for a murder: one o'clock on a dark and rainy Monday morning in early July. It had been a poor summer so far: so much wind and rain; more like winter.

The victim and his wife were sleeping.

The two men wore black balaclava masks. One of the men was big, with wide shoulders. The second man, tall and slim, gave the nod. The big man lowered a shoulder and crashed through the front door. They raced up the stairs, guns at the ready.

The victims were in the front bedroom, the one above the narrow street. They struggled to throw back the covers and leap out of bed, but it was too late. The two murderers charged in, spraying the room with bullets. The man and woman did not have a chance. They were dead before their bodies hit the wall. One of the men switched on the light, and they fired off a dozen more rounds, just to be sure.

In the bedroom across the hall, a boy was awake, deafened and terrified by the noise. He tried but could not move from his bed. Through his open door he could see masked men with guns. He smelled the smoke and powder from the guns, sharp like fireworks, like the house was on fire. He managed to get his feet on the floor but could not stand; his legs refused to support him. Though his ears were ringing from the violence of the explosions, he could hear the gunmen laughing and swearing, and he wanted to run but was tethered to his bed with fear. He was sure they had killed his mum and his da—for who could survive such firepower?—and now they would kill him. He had to get out of the house before they discovered him. But he couldn't move. His knees gave way and he slid off the bed onto the floor, unable to take his eyes off the men and their guns across the narrow hallway.

There were two of them. The big one reached up and pulled off his balaclava mask. The boy could see the man's red face and neck soaked with sweat, and his dark hair pointing up in damp spikes. There was a mole on his right cheek the size and color of an old Irish penny, large and brown. He even had a face like a mole, with a long nose and receding chin. The other man swore an order at him. The mole man quickly pulled the balaclava back over his head.

The boy took a deep breath and stood, holding onto his bed for support. He moved unsteadily to the window. His room looked out onto the backyard. The window was partially open at the bottom, enough for him to get his fingers under the wooden frame. He willed strength into his legs and arms and lifted carefully, trying not to make a noise. The casement was stiff, but fear, instead of melting his limbs, was now making him strong. The window slid upward until it reached the top and then screeched like a scalded cat. He heard the men shout, heard their boots pound the floor as they came for him. Hands reached out and grabbed him before he could jump out the window.

They had him.

He fell to the floor. The big man swung his boot and kicked him hard in the ribs. Behind the mask, his eyes looked like the cold dead eyes of a fish.

"He saw me!" growled the big man, staring with his dead fish eyes at the trembling boy. "He saw me, I know he did." He pointed his gun, finger tightening on the trigger.

The boy scrambled away, petrified, his back pressed against the wall.

The other man pushed the gun away quickly. "He's only a child!"

The big man reluctantly lowered the gun. "He's no child!
A filthy little Taig is all he is. I say we kill him and then get
the hell out of here before anyone sees us." He raised his
gun again.

The boy was anchored to the floor with fear. But he
knew that if he didn't move now—and move quickly—he
would be dead, like his parents. By a desperate act of will
he found enough courage to jerk his body upright and
throw himself out the open bedroom window. By the time
the big man had his finger pressed on the trigger ready to
fire, the boy was already sliding down the drainpipe like
a monkey. A broken neck was better than a chest full of
bullets. He fell off the drainpipe and landed in his mum's
muddy dahlia bed, more or less on his feet, then pitched
forward and rolled over, the way he had practiced at gymnastics. He jumped up and ran, expecting to feel the bullets thump into his back.

He did not feel the cold rain, only his fear.

Fear was his enemy. The thought flashed through his
mind that if he had used his brains the way his da always
said he should, if he had kept perfectly quiet and crawled
under the bed, then maybe they wouldn't have known he
was there, maybe they would have gone away and left him
alone. Fear, that's what it was; fear he would be slaugh-
tered, like his mum and his da.

He raced across the tiny backyard and out into the cobbled alleyway. He peered into the rainy darkness, his bare feet slapping on the cobblestones.

His mum and his da were dead, and he was running for his life. He could not hear the men coming after him, but he fled into the night, fled in fear, dressed only in his pajamas, his face covered in mud, tears and snot.

...*no time for a prayer*...

His name was Liam Fogarty, and he was twelve years old. He fled from the murderers, from the darkness toward the light, and was quickly out of the alley and onto his own street. He looked back. Nobody there. The killers hadn't chased him. Then he understood why: Most of the houses were showing lights in their windows. Neighbors disturbed from their sleep by the gunfire were standing in resolutely defensive postures out in the rain on the sidewalk. The women stood facing Liam's side of the street, arms boldly folded, while the men held make-do weapons in their fists: tire irons, wrecking bars, Hurley sticks and the like.

Neighbor Jack Cassidy shouted, "Liam! What happened?"

"They killed my mum and my da!" Liam screamed, pointing to his house, choking on his words. "They killed them!"

"How many of them?"

"Two..." He could hardly speak. His heart was pounding and he was breathless, not from the running so much as from fear...and rage.

Jack Cassidy grabbed him and pushed him to safety through his own front door and into his wife's arms. "Go inside, boy. Leave this to me."

Liam, still struggling for breath, watched Jack Cassidy gather the other men. "It's the Fogarty house," he yelled at them. They hurried across the street with their poor weapons.

Delia Cassidy wore a gray nightdress under her faded blue bathrobe. She took him by the arm. "Come inside, lovey, and take off the wet pajamas. There's dry things you can put on. Then I will make a wee drop of tea to warm you while I take a look at your foot. Come in, boy, God love you!"

He looked at the muddy splash of blood on his right foot, probably slashed by broken glass; the alleys were full of broken bottles. But that didn't matter; what mattered was the murderers had killed his mum and his da. Shot them in their bed, with no time for a prayer before they were sent to God.

The horror and shock of the past few minutes crashed suddenly in on him, and he felt his legs collapse.

When he again became aware of his surroundings, he sat up quickly. He had blacked out. Was that the way it happened when you died? One second you were here and the next you were gone? Was that the way it was for his mum and his da? Life—color, movement, smell, sound—then nothing?

He was lying on a couch, covered with a blanket, with Delia Cassidy hovering over him. About the same age as his mother and about the same thin build, she had short dark hair with strands of gray, gray eyes and a soft expression.

"Stay where you are, lovey. Drink this. It's a wee drop of tea. Drink it hot. Good for what ails you. And take this aspirin."

His head was thumping, and his ribs were sore where the big man with the mole had kicked him. He sat up and swallowed the aspirin with a sip of tea, aware now of the pain throbbing in his foot, but overwhelmed with the realization that his mum and his da were dead, their bodies shredded by monsters with guns. He found his voice. "I saw the…"

But he couldn't speak of it.

"Wait a bit. Drink your tea."

He did as he was told, sipping at the hot tea, his head throbbing. "My da and—"

"Yes, I know. Jack is over at your house. He will take care of things. Don't worry. I phoned the police as soon as we heard the shooting, but you know what they're like. It'll be at least an hour before they're here, if indeed they bother to come at all."

She called up the stairs, "Rory, run a hot bath for Liam. And fetch him something to put on." She handed Liam a towel. "Give yourself a long soak in the tub and a good rubbing with the towel. Rory will bring you something to put on."

He finished his tea.

"Do you feel able to stand?"

He nodded.

Rory was in Liam's class at St. Anthony's. He followed Liam into the bathroom and turned on the taps. Hot water pounded into the tub. "I'll bring you my new sweat suit," he said. "I've worn it only the once. It's warm."

"Thanks."

"Just try not to dribble your food onto it, boyo, okay? Here, have a Mint Imperial."

"Thanks." It was one of their favorite sweets. Liam popped the lozenge into his mouth. He was glad Rory wasn't asking questions. It was one of the things he liked about Rory: his quiet, unexcitable manner; the kidding around; the generosity, the "new" sweat suit from the thrift shop.

The two friends were alike in appearance: open faces, dark hair, fair skin with freckles, and a thin sinewy build. They were often mistaken for brothers. Their only real difference was their eyes: Liam's were a quizzical blue, Rory's a cool confident brown.

Liam's foot hurt. It was the same foot he had sprained a month ago at Youth Circus when he fell from the trapeze.

He sat in the hot bathtub and gingerly ran his fingers over the painful area on the pad of that same foot. It was swollen. But it didn't matter; it would mend. He was alive and not...

He hadn't seen his parents' bodies. The sight of them lying dead, broken and bleeding, would have driven him mad. Jack Cassidy and the other men were over there right now, in his mum and da's room. There was sure to be a great amount of blood.

His head throbbed. And his ribs. And his foot. He tried not to think of his mum and his da lying dead, tried not to think of the blood, but sank down as far as he could in the hot water and closed his eyes.

...safe with God...

"Now let me take a look at that foot," said Delia Cassidy once Liam was dressed in Rory's gray sweat suit and was back downstairs in the living room with a fresh cup of tea on the table beside him. The Cassidys were like everyone else in the neighborhood—they made tea fifty times a day.

He lay back and propped his leg up on the arm of the couch, dangling his foot for examination. His headache had almost gone; the aspirin and warm bath were doing their work. Rory inspected Liam's foot with great interest while his mother was removing tweezers from the boiling water on the stove. "Reminds me of the Androcles story," said Rory. "Androcles was the Greek slave feller who removed a thorn from a lion's paw, remember? The lion was very grateful. Soon after that, poor old Androcles ended up in the Roman arena, forced to fight for his life against a lion. Lion turned out to be the same one he had doctored. Lion was pleased to see his old friend. Instead of eating Androcles, he licked his face."

Delia Cassidy said, "Enough of that nonsense." She put on her glasses and peered at the wound, pressing around the swollen area gently with her thumbs. "There's a long sliver of glass. I can see it. Just you sit still, and I'll have it out in a jiff." She probed gently with the sterilized tweezers. It hurt like crazy. He wanted to pull his foot away, but he didn't move or cry out, just sat with his jaw clenched, absorbing the pain, knowing that the pain in his heart was much worse.

Jack Cassidy brought a rush of cold air with him as he came in the front door. He propped his Hurley stick against the wall, behind the door. "Ah, Liam! Your poor mum and da." He shook his head. "They're gone from us. If it had to be, then it's a blessing it was quick. They're safe with God."

"May they rest in peace," murmured Delia Cassidy.

Jack Cassidy came closer, watching his wife working the tweezers. "Your da was a strong leader here in Ballymurphy. Isn't that why they murdered him, for sure? It's them on the other side that want no peace, who are doing their utmost to drive us out of the North of Ireland altogether, or kill us all in our beds! May the black butchers who did this to your lovely family burn in hell!"

Delia Cassidy probed Liam's wound gently. "Your da had death threats. A gang of Protestant thugs had it in for him. Your mum didn't tell you, I know, but your da ignored the threats. 'They are out to kill you,' your mother told him. 'I'm in God's hands,' was all he said."

Jack Cassidy said, "Dan Fogarty is the fourth killed in as many weeks. Wasn't Con Begley shot down like a dog outside his own home in September? And the two Connolly brothers destroyed with a pipe-bomb through their letter box the week after?"

"Aye," said Delia Cassidy, "and it was only in March when that young mother in Lurgan, Rosemary Nelson, a solicitor, was killed by a bomb put under her car by the same murdering thugs."

Liam closed his eyes and thought about his mum and his da and their violent senseless deaths. He felt a terrible rage against their killers. He wanted to cry, but his heart and throat swelled and the tears would not come. Even the unbearable pain from Mrs. Cassidy's tweezers failed to help bring tears. What he really wanted was a gun in his hands and the killers at his mercy. He would..."Yeck!" That hurt!

Delia Cassidy winced. "Sorry, lovey."

Jack Cassidy said, "Did you get a good look at them, boy?"

The pain.

Without opening his eyes he said, "One of them. I saw his face."

"Who was he? Did you know him?"

He shook his head.

"There. I think I got it." Delia Cassidy held up a glass splinter. "I don't see anything else in there." She washed off the blood and painted iodine on the cut, then pressed a Band-Aid over it. "There. Now drink your cup of tea before it goes cold."

"Would you know the man again if you saw him?" asked Jack Cassidy.

Liam sat up and reached for his cup of tea. He nodded. He would never forget that face for as long as he lived: the mole on his cheek, the dead eyes, the mole-like face, the big hulking body.

"You can tell the police when they come. Describe the man to them."

Delia Cassidy rolled her eyes. "A fat lot of good that'll do," she muttered.

Jack Cassidy said, "If the police don't get them, then the IRA will, you can be sure of that."

Delia Cassidy said, "The IRA is as bad as the police and the soldiers. I wouldn't trust any of them. They're all a bunch of murderers, whichever side you're on. Wasn't it the IRA or the Real IRA, or whatever they call themselves, who planted a bomb that killed twenty-nine innocent folk in Omagh, not counting a pair of unborn twins? And crippled three hundred others? And they call themselves good Catholics! Don't be telling me about the IRA!"

Liam nursed his throbbing foot and sipped his tea.

Jack Cassidy cleared his throat. "About your mum and da," he said to Liam. "Mrs. Sheridan and Mrs. Coyne from down the street will stay with them until we can arrange to have them taken away. It would be better if we did it before any of your kinfolk see them. They'd be spared that at least."

Liam said nothing to Jack Cassidy, but he had no kinfolk, none he had ever met anyway. He knew his da had a much older brother who went to England when he was a teenager and never came back. He might even be dead.

Delia Cassidy sent her husband and Rory off to bed. "There's nothing to be done until the police come—if they come," she said to them. To Liam she said, "I'll make up a bed for you on the couch." She kneeled beside the couch and reached her arms around him. "Try to get some sleep," she said. "You will be safe here with us. Goodnight, lovey."

He disliked being hugged. His mum and his da were not touchy-feely people, and he wasn't used to it. But he let Delia Cassidy hug him, feeling nothing, feeling empty.

...the graveyard...

The Cassidy home was dark and hushed and filled with grief.

Over on the other side of the street, Liam's house was now a tomb. He pictured the two old women, Mrs. Sheridan and Mrs. Coyne, sitting with his mum and his da, "keeping vigil" Delia Cassidy had called it, in the bullet-wrecked, blood-soaked room. Across the hall, his own bedroom would be empty, its bedsheets and covers snarled, twisted and cold, and his circus posters—Charles Blondin crossing the Niagara Falls Gorge on a high-wire; Cirque du Soleil's trapeze artists, aerialists and clowns; the Great Wallendas' high-wire pyramid act; Bozo the Clown—left staring blindly into dark empty space.

The Cassidy household had gone back upstairs to bed except for Prissy the cat, curled up in a chair.

Liam lay restlessly on the couch. Every small noise in the house or on the street made him twitch nervously. His head still echoed with the sounds of death in his own home two hours earlier: the splintering blast of the front door as the killers launched their attack, the thump of boots on the stairs, the exploding guns, the smoke and reek of gunpowder. And the blood.

He tried to sleep, but his nerves and sinews were wide-awake. The mournful sound of wind and rain in the street outside fell on his ears like a dirge, as though Nature were lamenting the deaths of his beloved parents. Again, the thought of his mum and his da made him want to cry, but there was a dam in his throat that resisted tears. Fists and eyes clenched shut in desperation, he thrashed about on the narrow couch, twisting and turning, throwing off the covers. Sleep was impossible.

Sleep, like death.

A car went by outside with a splash of tires on the wet street. The wind moaned in the eaves. Rain pelted the window. The muted scream of a faraway ambulance siren joined with the melancholy sound of the wind.

The roar of a motorcycle assaulted the silence. It stopped, down at the end of the street, it sounded like. Nobody on the street owned a motorcycle, did they? He listened for the noise to start up again, but there was only the wind and the rain.

He reached down to the floor and retrieved the covers, but when they were back in place, he twisted and turned once more until they ended up back on the floor. He felt hot and clammy. He should take off the sweat suit, the bottoms anyway.

He could hear a sound, the faintest scrape of—what? A shoe or boot? There was someone outside. Ears straining, eyes staring at the shadows and patterns caused by the streetlight through the drawn curtains, he held his breath. There it was again! The night growl of a tomcat? Or the wind blowing a sodden cardboard box down the street?

Or maybe it was the mole man, coming for him. He waited, listening.

Silence. Then a faint scratching sound.

Fear skewered him. He started to tremble. Should he run upstairs and wake Jack Cassidy?

No, he decided. Instead he rose from the couch, painfully aware of his sore foot and his aching ribs, and moved as quietly as he could to the hallway where he found a pair of trainers with the laces tied. They belonged to Rory. A boy knows his best friend's shoes as well as he knows his own. He slipped them on, his injured foot more tender with the shoes. But he was ready to run if need be. He returned to the couch and sat on the edge, alert, listening and watching, trying to control the trembling of his shoulders.

It was too quiet. He held his breath, listening. The wind moaned in the eaves of the house. He rose and tiptoed to the kitchen and looked out the window. Because the house was small and narrow, the light from the streetlamp shone through the curtains at the front of the house and reflected off the upper part of the kitchen window at the back, preventing him from seeing out. He ducked his head and peered through the lower part of the window where it was dark. It was this sudden move that saved his life. The kitchen window shattered as the bullet meant for his head missed by the width of a hair, drilled through the wall behind him, sped through the living room, shattered the glass in the front window, ricocheted off a lamppost and flew impotently into the street.

Crackling with adrenaline, he turned and made a mad dash for the front door, fumbled the bolt open and sprinted out the door and down the street, away from the Cassidy house as fast as his grief-destroyed heart, lungs and legs would let him.

That had been close. He could now be lying dead on the kitchen floor, killed in an instant. You don't see it coming.

It's sudden. Without warning. You're alive—then you're dead. The end.

Like his mum and his da.

The Mole for sure.

He hadn't even felt the pain in his foot at first, but now it was like he was being stabbed with a knife.

The rain had eased off. The glistening street was all puddles and gurgling drains.

He heard the roar of a motorcycle starting up and glanced over his shoulder. The Mole on a motorcycle not far behind. He couldn't see the man's face, but there was no doubt in his mind that it was the Mole. Slipping and sliding in the puddles, he dodged into an alley, away from the streetlights, and kept going, sucking air. He ran out of the alley and into the next street over, heading toward Milltown Cemetery. He didn't need to look behind; the motorcycle was still roaringly there, dangerously close. He kept going, chest hammering. He turned into the next dark alley and stopped, pressing himself into invisibility in the nearest backyard doorway. He sucked air into his aching lungs and then tried to be quiet. Bike and rider approached his hiding place slowly and puttered past. He couldn't see the rider's face, but it had to be the Mole. Who else would be chasing him? Who else would be trying to kill him?

He counted to ten, took a deep breath, and ran back the way he had come, out onto the street again. Think! Think! Use your brains! Fool the killer somehow. But how? He crossed the Falls Road, plunged into another alley, and changed direction so that he was heading once again toward the cemetery. He had an idea! If he could get to the cemetery, he could hide in the Ludlow tomb, a sepulcher really, because there was no underground part. The gate on the front of the sepulcher was rusted and the padlock was broken. Inside the burying place rested several generations of the once wealthy Ludlow family who had made a fortune with their linen factory. But the sepulchre had been neglected for many years. Liam and Rory Cassidy and another boy, Sean Farrell, from St. Anthony's, had discovered last year that there was room enough inside—it was like a tiny stone house—for them to sit and smoke. If they were careful to close the gate and hang the broken padlock on the latch, then no one would ever guess they were there, sitting and smoking on the stone coffins of the Ludlow dead.

Not that any of them smoked regularly. It was merely a bit of rebellion to buy a packet of smokes and one or two bottles of Smithwick's once a month maybe, if they had the money, and sit around for an hour someplace, drinking and smoking and making believe they were cool and brilliant. His mum would kill him if she ever found out.

Not anymore she wouldn't. His mum was gone. Now he could do whatever he wanted. But who would be there to care?

He reached the high arch of the cemetery's main entrance—the sound of the motorcycle as it coursed up and down the alleys still behind him. Sometimes it roared. Sometimes it slowed and puttered.

To ease the pain in his foot, he tried walking on his heel.

The rain started again, thinly.

He turned up the collar of Rory's sweat suit and stood for a few seconds inside the gate to get his bearings. Everything looked diffcrent in the dark. The streetlights at the edge of the cemetery painted the nearest gravestones a grim yellow. He stumbled through the graveyard as quickly as he could in the rain and darkness, avoiding collision with tombs and gravestones, trying to remember the location of the Ludlow sepulchre. There was no light in this part. He had never been here at night in the dark. Fear of death from thc Mole overcame his fear of ghosts. He could still hear the gun exploding in his ear. The cemetery was scary. Stone angels and Celtic crosses loomed darkly over him like monsters, many of them as tall as fifteen feet.

At last, feeling his way, he found the place he was searching for. The sepulchre was high, like a narrow stone house. He snatched at the rusty padlock, unhooking it, swung open the gate, closed it behind him, stepped across a narrow strip of weeds and was quickly inside out of the rain. He felt his way along the wall, and when he came to the first stone coffin at ground level—most were on stone shelves—he sat. It was good to take the weight off his foot.

He had found the hideaway only just in time. He could hear the putter-putter of the searching motorcycle in the cemetery.

He was scared. He was alone. And he was sitting on a stone coffin.

"It's not a coffin; it's a casket," Sean Farrell had said the first time they sat inside. "That's what they're called these days, a casket. And this place is called a crypt. The cat crept in the crypt and crapped." He laughed.

"A crypt is below ground," said Rory. Rory was a big reader. "This frightful edifice, you ignoramus, is a sepulchre."

Liam wished Rory and Sean were with him right now. Anyway, he was sitting on a coffin, and it didn't matter a tinker's hoot what other names it had. A coffin is a coffin, plain and simple. With a dead body inside. And Rory and Sean were not there with him, play-acting and cracking jokes and blowing cigarette smoke into the dank gloomy air. They used to wonder if there was a wooden coffin inside the stone one. And inside the wooden coffin...? Like a set of Russian dolls, smaller and smaller, until finally a tiny box and a withered Ludlow homunculus (Rory's word) the size of a dried raisin…

It was cold and wet. July? Might as well live at the North Pole as live in Belfast.

The motorcycle noise went away. After a while it came back. It stopped near Liam's hiding place. Was the Mole coming to check the sepulchre? Why would the Mole stop at this particular one of the many sepulchres throughout the cemetery? He strained his ears listening for the sound of a hand on the padlock. Nothing. The motorcycle noise started again. Then it went away.

Silence.

He sat in the dark, arms folded over his shivering chest, legs pressed tight together, and waited for daylight as he tried not to think of the many Ludlow ghosts around him, lying in their cold coffins, or hovering over his head, preparing to stop his grief-destroyed heart with fright.

...lighting a candle...

He was too scared to sleep. Besides, it was cold in the sepulchre. The pain throbbed in his foot. It was the ankle of the same foot he had sprained the time he fell off the trapeze at YC, or Youth Circus.

A Protestant boy named Timmy Banks is the anchor. He is holding the rope attached to Liam's safety harness. Timmy stumbles and loses his grip. The rope races through the pulley. Liam, still twelve feet above the ring floor, drops like a bomb and twists his ankle. The pain is excruciating.

Timmy is eleven. He cries.

Nicole Easterbrook, another Protestant, carefully, tenderly removes Liam's shoe while her friend Grace Newton runs for the director. Rory is there. He helps Nicole peel off Liam's sock.

Liam and Rory became members of the Belfast Community Youth Circus after being on their waiting list for a whole year. Catholic and Protestant kids work and train together on Saturdays, and sometimes Sundays. The circus school is under the directorship of the severe Madame Dubois and has a hundred young members with a waiting list of as many more. Started originally as a way of creating friendship and harmony between young Catholics and Protestants, it continues to encourage kids to forget their differences and work and train together. For children whose parents are unemployed, the fees are waived.

Accidents sometimes happen. Sprained ankles and wrists are not at all unusual.

Rory helps Liam hop to Madame Dubois' car. Liam sits in front next to the director. Rory gets into the car and sits in the back. The two boys are stiff with shyness.

Madame Dubois drives to the hospital, and the foot is X-rayed and bandaged. Then she takes the two boys home. Not a word is exchanged between them in the ten minutes it takes for Madame Dubois to drive them home through west Belfast's mean streets. To Liam, nursing his throbbing ankle, the journey seems to take forever, not because of the pain but because of the silent authority of the director's straight no-nonsense back.

Supported by Rory and escorted by the director, Liam hops into the house. Liam and Rory are still dumb from the car ride, so Madame Dubois introduces herself to Liam's mum and da. Liam can see that they are temporarily stunned by her French accent and haughty polished manner. She does not offer her hand.

"Mr. Fogarty? Mrs. Fogarty? I am Madame Dubois, director of the Youth Circus. Your son had a small accident, yes?" She hands Liam's shoe and sock to Mr. Fogarty, who stares at them stupidly while Madame Dubois continues. "It is nothing to be too concerned about. A sprained ankle is all, but he will be forced to rest awhile, I'm afraid." She speaks, without so much as a nod or a smile, with the air of an expert on sprained ankles.

By now Liam is lying on the couch with his foot up on the arm and, though suffering from the pain of his swollen ankle, can see that his parents, like all the circus students, are awed by the director's take-charge personality.

Rory stands helplessly by.

Liam's mum fetches a bag of frozen peas, wraps it in a towel and shapes it to fit around Liam's ankle.

His da recovers from his astonishment. "It was remarkable kind of you to drive him to the hospital and bring him home, Madame Dubois. Will you stay for a wee cup of tea?

Sure you will; I will put on the kettle."

His mum, holding the frozen peas to Liam's ankle, looks up at Madame Dubois. "Please sit, won't you?"

Madame Dubois flutters her hands. "Thank you, no. I must be on my way." She nods at Liam. "It was an awkward fall, but soon you will return to your training."

His da says, "An awkward colt often becomes a speedy horse, isn't that right, Madame Dubois?"

Madame Dubois stares at him blankly.

His da smiles. "An old Irish saying."

His mum stands. "Thanks again for bringing him home."

"The boy will soon be on his feet again, don't worry," says his da.

Madame Dubois leaves without another word.

They love the circus. When they are kids, soon after Liam moves to the Ballymurphy neighborhood, he and Rory sneak into a circus in Belfast, ducking through the turnstiles after Rory's well-aimed stink bomb diverts the ticket collector's attention.

Soon after that, Liam discovers *Trapeze*, an old 1956 film, in the video store on Springfield Street. Hollywood hero Burt Lancaster plays the part of a famous trapeze artist named Mike Ribble. Liam and Rory rent the film as often as they can afford it. They think it is brilliant.

Black night melted into dark gray gloom.

Liam crawled out of the sepulchre shivering and looked about him with bleary eyes. No rain. He hooked the padlock back on the gate with cold trembling fingers. When he was sure no one was watching, he started walking quickly to get his blood flowing, to shake out the cramps in his legs and warm himself up. His sore foot felt tender inside the shoe, and his ribs ached on the left side where he had been kicked. His walking slowed and he began to limp. Motorcycle tire tracks muddied the grass and the many flat gravestones; vases and jars of flowers were shattered and scattered on the ground. He limped out the gate, pausing first to make sure the coast was clear. No motorcycle; no sign of the Mole.

He made his way back to the Cassidy house and beat on the door with his fist.

Delia Cassidy, in pink sweater and jeans, jerked the door open. "Ah! Thank God you're all right, lovey. We thought you were killed. Or kidnapped. Thanks be to heaven you're safe! Come in, for God's sake. Come in, boy. The police were over at your house and then they came here. Two of the Royal Ulster Constabulary's finest. They sent a car looking for you. Come in, come in." Her husband and

Rory stood behind her, wide-eyed and anxious.

He limped into the kitchen while Delia Cassidy called the police.

Breakfast time. Delia Cassidy had noticed him limping. She finished calling the police and sat him down. Jack Cassidy placed a hot mug of tea in his hands to warm him.

"The police are on their way," said Delia Cassidy.

Liam told them what had happened and about his night in the Ludlow tomb. Delia Cassidy gathered her first-aid things together. "It's obvious what happened here," she said. "Didn't we hear the gun? And see the destruction caused down here? Thanks be to God you weren't killed like your poor mum and da, God save them both."

"It's clear you can't stay here tonight," said Jack Cassidy.

Rory's eyes were wide with worry. "This Mole feller, he knows where you are, Liam. He'll annihilate you for sure."

That was Rory. Never used a short word if a long one would do.

Delia Cassidy had her tweezers ready. "Lie on the couch and I'll just take a wee look at that foot again."

Liam lay on the couch with his foot dangling over the arm, as before, trying not to cry out while Delia Cassidy removed the Band-Aid and probed his foot gently with her tweezers again. "What will the boy do to be safe?" she asked her husband over her shoulder.

"Go to the IRA," said Rory, butting in. "They'll protect him."

Delia Cassidy looked up sharply. "Hush your mouth with the IRA. The only thing they're good for is killing innocent people."

Jack Cassidy shook his head. "The boy must go to the police. There's no other way, or this time tomorrow he will be stone dead for sure."

"Are you mad?" said Delia Cassidy. "Are you out of your mind, man? The police are worse than the IRA! Aren't the police all Protestants? I wouldn't trust them with the cat. They'd be just as likely to hand the boy over to a gang of Protestant thugs! Hold still, Liam. There's the tiniest wee bit left in there and I almost have it."

"Ouch!" The biting pain made it hard for him to hold still.

"Aye," said Jack Cassidy, "but there's a few Catholics in the police force—not many, you're right, only a few percent maybe—but the lad will be safer with them than here with us, a sitting target for those murdering butchers. He might not be so lucky next time."

Delia Cassidy held up the tweezers for Liam's inspection. "There! See? The last piece, I'm sure. I'll put on a fresh Band-Aid and you'll be as fit as a butcher's dog, as my father used to say. It might be a good idea to walk on your heel whenever you can, so the Band-Aid doesn't come off.

We don't want dirt getting in there and causing infection."

Jack Cassidy said, "Eat some breakfast, boy, and then get a bit of rest before the police get here."

Liam ate a small bowl of cereal but couldn't face the plate of toast, butter and marmalade in front of him. He stretched himself out on the couch. It felt good to lie down. He was exhausted. Everything ached.

Delia Cassidy said, "The police will take their own sweet time." She put on her raincoat. "I'm away to the church. I'll not be long. Back before the police get here. I want to light two candles for the repose of the souls of your poor unfortunate mum and da."

Candles.

Liam closed his eyes. Delia Cassidy was like his mother, and most of the women in the parish, lighting candles in St. Anthony's church, pushing them into the spiked candleholders, crossing themselves, bowing their heads in prayer. Fiona Fogarty had made it a habit, dropping a coin into the collection box and lighting a candle after Mass every Sunday without fail.

"Why do you always light a candle, Mum?"

He is nine years old.

"It's for a private intention."

"What's a private attention?"

"Private means it's a secret between me and God. Lighting a candle is a prayer asking God for something."

"What are you asking God for, Mum?"

"Never you mind. It's private. That's why it's called a private intention."

He watches the way her dark hair falls into her eyes, watches how she flicks it back with a shake of her head. Her hazel eyes are permanently anxious, it seems, because she has to make do with very little money. Liam is old enough to understand that it is always a struggle for his mother to find the rent and put meals on the table and clothes on their backs. And yet she never misses her candle conversation with God after Sunday Mass, even though coins are scarce.

She bends her head in prayer. Then she crosses herself and the ceremony is over for another week.

Liam said, "Could I ask for a private attention too? Would I have to light a candle? I could ask God for a bicycle. Do you think He would listen?"

"It's intention, not attention. God is always listening. No, the candle is not important; you can ask for whatever you want. But that doesn't necessarily mean you will get it."

"If the candle isn't important, why do you light one then?"

"It's a symbol, that's all, a symbol of hope and remembrance." She thinks for a second. "And gratefulness," she adds.

"What's a symbol, Mum?"

The next Sunday he stands at the altar without lighting a candle and asks God for a bicycle. Six months go by before his da brings home a second-hand bicycle from "The Spinning Wheel," John Joe Murphy's sports shop in Ballymurphy.

"You're right," Liam tells his mother. "I didn't even need to light a candle."

...last day together...

Their last day together:

He walks with his mother to the ten o'clock Sunday morning Mass, her last. As they approach St. Anthony's, he hangs back, looking for his friends Rory and Sean. He no longer sits and kneels with his mother in a pew; he is much too old for that. Instead he joins Rory and Sean at the back of the church where they stand with the latecomers, and then, when no one is looking, slip away to share an illegal cigarette behind the presbytery wall.

His da never goes to church services. He spends the last Sunday morning of his life over at Maloney's Pub earning a bit of extra money helping Declan Maloney install new toilet bowls in the two lavatories.

In the evening, after Liam gets home from Youth Circus, they sit down to one of Liam's favorite dinners: tuna casserole. Canned tuna is cheap and so is packaged pasta. Throw in a handful of chopped broccoli, finish with a golden cheese crust, and enjoy.

They talk. His da asks Liam about his day at Youth Circus and about his friend Nicole. Liam blushes. His mum rescues him by asking his da about his day working at Maloney's Pub, and his da asks her if there is any more of the casserole left in the dish because a man gets remarkable hungry on his knees all day installing toilets.

Their last meal together.

For his mum and his da, it is their last meal ever.

He lay on the Cassidy couch with his eyes closed, foot throbbing, ribs aching. Thinking about his mum and his da made him want to cry, but he couldn't cry. It was like there was something inside that was wound up tight and, no matter how hard he tried, he couldn't let it go.

Rory answered the telephone. "It's the police," he told Liam. "They're on their way. Ten minutes."

The police arrived. Just one, in plain clothes. He did not take off his hat. He asked Liam a few questions about the men who had killed his parents. Liam told him what he knew. The policeman didn't ask about the man who had shot at him through the Cassidy kitchen window. Instead he told Liam to put on his shoes and coat and come with him to the police station; Inspector Osborne wanted to ask him a few questions.

Delia Cassidy, back from the church, said to Liam, "Jack and I will go with you. Rory will mind the house." She packed clothing and a sandwich in a packsack. "You had better take this. I wouldn't be a bit surprised if the police decide to keep you out of sight for a while."

The policeman drove them to the police station.

The small office was crowded with only five people: Inspector Osborne, Jack and Delia Cassidy, a pleasant-faced young woman named Miss Tovey from the Children's Welfare office, and Liam.

Osborne. Protestant name, Liam guessed.

When the inspector had finished introducing everyone, he sat behind his desk and turned his attention to Liam, seated in front of him on a hard chair.

The expression on the face of Delia Cassidy, seated beside her husband and to the side of Inspector Osborne's desk, seemed to say, "Never trust a policeman."

Inspector Osborne was a tall man, slim, with blue eyes, short gray hair, and a neat ginger mustache stained by the nicotine of many cigarettes. He wore a smart bottle-green police uniform with a white shirt and black tie.

Liam hated uniforms: They usually spelled trouble. This uniformed police inspector intimidated him.

The inspector tried to put Liam at ease, smiling encouragingly. "Now, Liam, tell me what happened exactly as you remember it. Take your time. You were asleep, you say, when two men broke into your home."

Delia Cassidy said, "Filthy butchers. Animals are what they were, not men."

The inspector raised an eyebrow. "Liam?"

"What kind of men would massacre two innocent people in their bed?" asked Delia Cassidy.

The inspector turned to her politely. "I would like to hear the story from the boy, Mrs. Cassidy, if you don't mind."

Liam was very tired. He talked haltingly. Inspector Osborne listened attentively, quietly interrupting to ask an occasional question.

After Liam was finished, the inspector, amid interruptions from Delia Cassidy, asked him further questions about the two killers, especially the big one who had taken off his mask.

Liam described him.

"You say that this same man, the one with the mole, later tried to kill you in the Cassidy home?"

"The window will need to be replaced," said Delia Cassidy, "and the wall is destroyed with…"

"Please, Mrs. Cassidy!" Inspector Osborne glared at her.

Liam said, "He shot at me through the window. I ran out of the house, and he came after me on a motorbike. I spent the night hiding in the cemetery."

"The individual who shot at you, did you see his face?"

"No."

"The man on the motorcycle, did you see his face?"

"No."

"Who else could it be?" asked Delia Cassidy. "Wasn't it the devil himself?"

The inspector's patience had come to an end. "Mrs. Cassidy, I will have to ask you to be quiet, or you must wait outside. How can I interview the boy if you insist on interrupting?"

"Hmmph!" said Delia Cassidy.

"So, Liam, you cannot actually say that the man who fired at you and the man who chased you on the bike was the man with the mole on his face, the same man who was responsible for the deaths of your parents?"

"No, but it was him, I'm sure."

The inspector turned to include Jack Cassidy and Miss Tovey. "When it comes to proving something, when it comes to saying that you know it was the same man, that you recognized him, well, the courts are very reluctant…"

Liam said, "You don't believe me?"

"Yes, Liam, I believe you. I think it was the same man. But thinking and knowing for certain are horses of a different color, you see?"

"No, I don't see."

The inspector sighed. "Liam, you are obviously in great danger. If you stay where you are, then he is sure to try again." He turned to the Cassidys. "You must leave things in my hands. I will take care of the boy. You cannot protect him. Your home is a dangerous place for him now. I want him under police protection. Do you agree, Miss Tovey?"

Miss Tovey nodded. "Of course, Inspector. Liam comes first. We must protect him."

The inspector directed the same question at the Cassidys.

Jack Cassidy said, "It's the only way."

Inspector Osborne turned back to Liam. "I want to send you to a safe house."

Liam must have looked alarmed because Miss Tovey, with a sympathetic smile, said, "It's a secret house in the city, Liam. You will be perfectly safe there, I promise."

Inspector Osborne said, "You will live there until we have the killer in jail. Miss Tovey is right. You will be safe there. Nobody will know where you are. Nobody. We tell no one, not even Mr. and Mrs. Cassidy. Not even your family."

"Got no family now."

The inspector's eyebrows shot up in surprise. "No grandparents?"

Liam shook his head.

"No aunts or uncles?"

"Nobody."

Delia Cassidy looked at her husband with raised eyebrows. Jack Cassidy nodded to her.

"He has no one but us," said Delia Cassidy.

The inspector pulled a face and bit his lower lip. "In any case, the only ones who know where you are will be myself, the police driver, and the two staff members who work in the house, Fergus and Moira Grogan. They are entirely trustworthy." He stopped and narrowed his eyes. "They would be like an aunt and uncle. How do you feel about that?"

Liam shrugged. He had never had an aunt or an uncle, so he didn't know what they would be like.

Inspector Osborne stood. "I will have you taken to the safe house. But first I'd like you to spend a few minutes with our identification man. He will work up a picture on the computer from your description of the man with the mole." The inspector fingered his mustache and said to the Cassidys. "He is sure to belong to one of the militant Loyalist gangs. If all goes well we should have these killers in custody by the end of the month." To Liam he said, "Do you think you can pick your mole man out of a line-up?"

"That's when you line up a bunch of people and—"

"He wouldn't see you. You would be in a separate room looking through a one-way window. What do you say? Could you do it?"

"Sure."

"Good boy. And if we can persuade him to talk, we will have the other one too."

...safe house...

The computer identification procedure over, he waited in the inspector's office for a car to take him to the safe house. Jack and Delia Cassidy sat with him; Miss Tovey had gone. The inspector was out of the room.

Delia Cassidy said, "Tell the boy, Jack."

Jack Cassidy put an arm round Liam's shoulders. "When this is all over, when they catch these killers, we want you to know that our home is your home. It will be waiting for you. Understand?"

Liam nodded. "Thanks," was all he could say.

Jack Cassidy handed him a worn leather wallet. "Here. Keep this. It has a little money in it for emergencies and our telephone number, in case you forget it. Call us if there is anything you need, and we will see you get it. Will you do that?"

Liam nodded, not trusting himself to speak.

The police inspector came back and the Cassidys said goodbye. Delia Cassidy said, "The inspector promised me you will want for nothing at the safe house: new clothing, soap, toothbrush, books to read, everything." She hugged him. "Be brave, lovey." Jack Cassidy smiled sadly, started to say something, but stopped and squeezed Liam's shoulder. They left.

Liam and Inspector Osborne were alone in the office. The inspector sat down behind his desk. "The car will be here any minute." He smiled.

Inspector Osborne seemed an okay person, but Liam still did not quite trust him: He was a policeman, after all, and a Protestant. A Protestant Loyalist: loyal to the queen of England. Which was the same as English, not Irish. You couldn't be English and Irish: one or the other but not both. But he felt less intimidated, especially if he made an effort to see the man and not the uniform. He said, "Why did they kill my mum and da? Do you know? They never did anything to hurt anyone. They were good people. It makes no sense."

"You're right. It makes no sense, Liam. Your parents are two of five retaliation killings in the past week. We think a paramilitary group is out to revenge the killing last month of John Spencer in the Maze prison. You have heard of the Maze prison?"

"Yes."

"Spencer was a Loyalist paramilitary chief, sent to jail for his crimes. An IRA prisoner stabbed Spencer to death in the prison yard."

"But my da had nothing to do with that!"

The inspector sighed. "True. Retaliation killings make no sense. Those seeking revenge don't really care who they kill as long as it is one of the 'enemy.' Do you understand?"

Liam thought he understood. So the killings were more or less random. They could have targeted any Catholic; it would have made no difference to the killers.

Inspector Osborne said, "Dan Fogarty was well known. He was a community leader and a peacemaker. Everyone knew your father. The price of fame in Belfast is sometimes death."

That was what Jack Cassidy had said, Liam remembered. There were Prods who did not want peace, who only wanted the Catholics out of the North of Ireland.

Liam hated the killers. The hate was a deadly cold snake inside him, aching to strike. His father was the best of all fathers, the best in the whole world, the sort of man who wouldn't do a bit of harm to anyone, always happy, even when he had nothing much to be happy about. Liam knew only a little about his da's activities, about how he spoke out for the rights of the poor and unemployed in the North of Ireland, no matter whether they were Prods or Catholics; he knew that his father saw no important differences between them. They were all doing their best, he always said, Protestants and Catholics alike, to find work and bring up their families. It was just a few who were to blame for the violence and the hatred, a handful of ignorant thugs who knew no better.

His da tried to reason quietly with young hotheads who believed that tit-for-tat violence in the North of Ireland must go on day after day, month after month, year after year, who believed that things would never change. "There's an old Irish saying," his da would say to them with a smile. "If nothing ever changed, there would be no butterflies."

He tried to see the good in everyone; he was a man who seldom lost his temper—not like Liam's mother Fiona who became upset and angry every time someone was killed by a gang of terrorists, or by a car bomb, or by the police, or by the British army soldiers. Her anger expressed itself in tears and explosive wails of distress that left her eyes red. His da would comfort her in his calm, quiet voice, and a reassuring arm around her shoulders.

He would have his own room, Inspector Osborne said.

The police driver drove him around the city, north, east, south and west, before finally pulling up at a big old house. By now it was dark. "Got to make sure we're not followed," the driver explained to Liam, who was half-asleep on the backseat. It had been a long day, and with no sleep last night in the Ludlow sepulchre, he was exhausted. They entered the house quietly by the back door, Liam carrying his small backpack.

The Grogans seemed okay, but not a bit like he'd imagined an aunt and uncle, serious and stiff instead, but that was to be expected of people whose job it was to run a secret police house where there were so many rules. The man, Fergus, wasn't a member of the police, but he acted like he was. He was a mixture of bossy and friendly, an older man, balding and stockily built, with a narrow brown mustache. He already knew about Liam's parents. "Sorry for your trouble," he muttered as he shook Liam's hand with a thick paw.

His wife Moira was ordinary looking: medium build, light brown hair with some gray, a chain-smoker. She nodded at him. "Sorry for your trouble," she murmured but didn't shake his hand, flashing him a tight little smile instead.

The house was twice the size of Liam's house in Ballymurphy, and it had been updated, with fresh paint and newly sanded and varnished hardwood floors, though Liam noticed none of this.

Fergus sat Liam down at the kitchen table and went over the rules with him. He was so tired he could hardly keep his eyes open to read the big capital letters on lined yellow foolscap paper. Fergus said, "You cannot go out. That's number one. You stay inside and you don't show yourself to anyone. You got it?"

He nodded.

"You don't leave this house under any circumstances. Never ever, okay? You reading me?"

Liam nodded.

"There's a lavatory in the backyard. But it's not for you. Why not?"

"It's outside."

"Good. You're listening. Your room is at the back, upstairs. Moira will take you up after dinner. The bathroom is right next-door. That's the lavatory you use. Next: You leave nothing belonging to you downstairs where someone might see it. As far as everyone in the neighborhood is concerned, the only ones living here are me and the missus.

"Next: You do whatever me and Moira tells you to do. That includes washing dishes, helping keep the house clean and tidy, looking after your own room and your own stuff and your own laundry—Moira will show you how to work the washing machine. Okay?"

He nodded once again. All he wanted to do was lay his head down on the table and go to sleep.

"You eat whatever Moira cooks for you, or you go without, understand? This ain't the Europa International Hotel. Unless there's something you really hate, which you better tell me about now."

He shrugged.

"Okay, no hates. Now, the telephone. You're allowed to make one call a day. That's it, period. One call only. When you make a call, you got to tell me or Moira first before you make it, and we got to know who you're calling, you got that? Any incoming calls go through me or Moira."

He stared at the man, trying to keep his eyes open.

"And you don't give out any information about this place when you're on the blower. That means you don't tell no one where it is or what it looks like. You tell them nothing that could lead anyone here, got it? You tell no one my name or Moira's name, nothing. You understand? Grogan isn't our real name anyway. Get it? Your calls will be monitored.

"Now, the telly. You can use the telly in the living room as much as you want before nine o'clock at night. After that you go to your room, and you stay upstairs until six the next morning. Breakfast is at seven. If we look in on you during the evening, we'll always knock. When you use the bathroom, you don't lock the door. Don't worry, no one's going to barge in on you, but leave the lock off, okay? We don't want no accidents. There's books and magazines in the house. Just help yourself to whatever you need. Take 'em up to your room if you like. If you have problems, then you come to me or Moira. Any questions?"

Liam yawned. "Sounds like a prison."

"You better believe it."

Dinner was spaghetti and meatballs, but he didn't really see it and wasn't the slightest bit hungry. With so little sleep last night, he was too tired even to pick at the food. There was no dessert, just tea. When they were finished, Liam carried his plate out to the kitchen and emptied his uneaten food into the rubbish bag.

The Grogans saw he was tired and excused him from kitchen duty. He grabbed his backpack. Moira took him upstairs and showed him the bathroom and his bedroom.

He shut the door and took off his things. He didn't bother to unpack. There were fresh pajamas on the bed, but he didn't bother to put them on. He crawled under the covers and, in less than a minute, he was fast asleep.

...exhaustion...

He slept fitfully and dreamed of splintered doors and heavy boots rushing up stairs and crashing gunfire and voices screaming.

He slept through breakfast the next morning and did not hear the knocking on his door, did not see his door pushed open a few inches while Moira Grogan peeped in on him, and then close the door and let him sleep.

He slept the day away, such was his exhaustion, and did not wake until the evening. He had trouble remembering where he was. Then his first thought was that his mum and his da were dead, and he was alone.

They were not so very old; his da was thirty-seven or eight, and his mum was about the same, or maybe a year or two younger. Most people these days lived into their seventies or eighties. But not Dan and Fiona Fogarty: They were dead before forty. Their lives were over. It was impossible to grasp. He felt numb just thinking about it.

It was still early morning. What time? He looked over at the digital clock with its glowing red figures: six-thirteen. He looked closer, saw the PM sign, and puzzled over it for a few seconds. Either the clock was wrong, or he had slept a full night and day, almost twenty-four hours.

He got up, showered, and was sitting at the dinner table by seven. Fergus was reading his newspaper at the table. He nodded at Liam and went back to his paper. Moira was in the kitchen. "I wondered if you would be down," she said. "You've been asleep all day."

Asleep all day? Then he should be feeling rested; instead he felt weak, heavy, numb. Stunned.

The phone rang. Fergus answered. "It's for you." He held the receiver out to Liam.

"Liam? It's Inspector Osborne. How are you settling in?"

"Fine."

It wasn't private. They could hear him talk to Inspector Osborne through the doorless arch to the living room. He knew they were listening; hadn't Fergus said they would monitor the calls?

"The funeral is set for tomorrow, Thursday."

"Thanks."

"I thought you should know."

"Yes."

"Father Monaghan will be saying a requiem mass. The burial is in the morning at Milltown Cemetery."

"Right."

"If you want, I could send a car and a bodyguard to take you to the funeral and then take you back again. But I don't think you should go. It could be dangerous. That's my advice. You would be better off staying right where you are and not showing yourself. The killer might be expecting you to show up."

"Yes."

He must have stopped listening after that because he remembered no more of the conversation, didn't even remember hanging up.

Dinner was a blur. He ate very little. The funeral was all he could think about. The Grogans had very little to say at the table. They asked him no questions. There was no more said about his day in bed. Liam noticed nothing of Fergus reading *The Irish News*—the Nationalist, Catholic newspaper—its pages spread out over most of the table, nor Moira chewing her food and staring unseeingly over Fergus's head at a picture of Pope John Paul II hanging over the mantel. They were Catholics, he thought. He sat in a trance, seeing two coffins carried to Milltown Cemetery in the pouring rain.

Moira helped clear the table. She showed Liam where everything was. Then she left him to wash and dry the dishes and put them away in the cupboards, which he did like a robot, automatically, unthinkingly, and didn't notice the Grogans moving to the living room, Fergus to continue reading his newspaper, Moira to watch the telly.

After clean up, Liam grabbed a couple of books from the living room, said goodnight and climbed the stairs to his room.

He had been too tired last night to take much notice of his room, but now he saw that it was quite bare: a single bed with sheets, blanket and a yellow cover—now rumpled from his long sleep—a night table with the digital clock, no chest of drawers. There was nothing else in the room, no pictures, no plants, no ornaments, nothing. The only light was a bare bulb hanging from the center of the room.

The air in the room smelled stale from his long sleep; he noticed that the window was closed. He tried to open it by gripping the two metal handles at the bottom and lifting the frame, but it would not budge no matter how hard he tried. Then he noticed that the window glass was painted over with a dark brown paint. No one could look in or out.

Then he noticed a small clear square where paint had been scratched off, in the bottom left-hand corner. He kneeled and peeped out, but there wasn't much to see, only the rain.

It would soon be time for bed again, but how could he sleep after sleeping away a whole day? He lay on his bed, back against the headboard, and looked at the title of one of his books: *Space Monsters*. Why go all the way out to space when there was an abundance of monsters right here in Belfast? He opened the book to the first story and started reading.

He hadn't read ten words before his eyes wandered from the page. He was alone. The house was quiet.

He had never been alone before, not like this. No da or mum to talk to. Not even a friend, like Rory or Sean. Or Nicole, his new friend at Youth Circus.

He was completely alone.

He became aware of the beat of his heart and the sound of his breathing. He could hear the tiny creaks and clicks of the house, caused by temperature changes in the walls and pipes.

He put down his book and changed into the pajamas provided by the Grogans. Might as well. He wasn't going anywhere. He wished he had his own red-striped flannel ones, bought by his mum.

He sat on the floor and explored the Band-Aid on his foot with his fingers: still stuck firmly; hadn't peeled off in the shower; no pain, just a little tenderness. He stayed seated on the floor, staring at the wall. He stared at the wall for so long he lost track of time. He became aware that he was cold. He climbed under the bed covers and tried reading again, but his eyes were too tired to focus on the small print and, besides, reading seemed to be something he used to do, once, when he'd had a family, when the world made some sense. How could he relax enough to read when his mother and father were so suddenly gone from him, and he was alone in a strange house?

He put the book down and closed his eyes.

He knew what the funeral would be like tomorrow morning. There would be a masked IRA guard around the coffins. They would be carrying guns. It was normal. There would be soldiers in their armored vehicles and police in their "meat wagons"—armor-plated Land Rovers. There would be crowds of people.

He wouldn't be there.

After the funeral, they would all go away.

A lump came to his throat. He tried to think of something else instead, like school, or gymnastics, or the circus, anything to stop thinking of his mum and his da lying dead in coffins, shot to death, or their funeral tomorrow.

...Youth Circus...

Normally on a Wednesday evening he would be with Rory and Sean at the local Ballymurphy Gymnastics Club where they trained two evenings a week. It was boys mainly, though sometimes there might be a girl or two. Then on Saturdays, Liam and Rory trained at the Belfast Community Youth Circus as first-year students, taking the bus to the new "purpose-built" circus building in the city center. The circus "ring" was actually a rectangular gymnasium with adjacent stretch and exercise rooms and offices.

There were girls at the Youth Circus. Two of them were friends: Nicole Easterbrook and Grace Newton, from a middle-class Protestant area of Belfast where there were no bombs or shootings. Both girls, close to Liam and Rory's age but already with a year of circus experience, were fearless performers with amazing moves. Liam had never realized that girls could be so powerful, could own so much fire. Local Ballymurphy girls played football, and were good, strong players, but were slow and timid in comparison to Nicole and Grace. Who would have guessed there were girls in Belfast who didn't whisper and giggle, who were fast and fearless, who were wirewalkers, tumblers, gymnasts, beginning trapeze artists, who made your mouth drop open in astonishment and admIRAtion as you watched them?

Madame Dubois, the director, was very strict. Catholic and Protestant kids worked and trained together. They had to get along; otherwise, they were kicked out. One of the kids, a boy named William, was from the Protestant Shankill area, the section separated from Liam's Falls Road section by the Peace Line Wall. William always wore long-sleeved shirts because his arms, Liam recently discovered, were tattooed "Kill all Taigs," a message seen on walls and doors all over west Belfast as "KAT." The opposing message was also well represented: "KAP."

When it came to all-round gymnastics at the local club—floor exercises and apparatus—parallel bars, horizontal bar, pommel horse, balance beam—Rory Cassidy was the superior athlete. Coach Cannon was preparing him for the Belfast Junior Finals in the spring.

Liam didn't mind being second best, or third best for that matter. His da had put him straight when Liam had come home from gymnastics one evening a bit depressed because things hadn't gone so well. He had been clumsy and slow. "You're not focusing, Fogarty," the gymnastics coach had yelled at him.

"I'll never be as good as Rory," he told his da. "Or as good as Nicole and Grace at Youth Circus."

"There's an old Irish saying," his da consoled him. "'The forest would be terrible silent if no birds sang except those that sang the best.'"

The time spent circus training was what Liam loved most. Last summer he was accepted for a ten-day circus camp, funded by the Community Youth Circus. Brilliant it was. Ten days of heaven. Though his main skill was acrobatics, he wore a safety harness to train with trapeze artists. Then there were clown workshops and instruction in stilt walking and juggling as well as unicycling and walking on the hands. Students at the workshops, those who were serious about circus as a profession, knew that one day they would have to choose a specialty of their own, but circus performers were expected to acquire as many performance skills as possible. Liam's choice of specialty, he decided, would be either trapeze artist or clown.

Toward the end of the summer camp, everyone had to put on an individual clown act. The goal was to make the others in the class laugh. "Wear something funny," the director told them. Liam chose to wear his favorite red-striped pajamas, plastic red nose and red-striped face, and he clowned it up on a unicycle. He acted the part of an incompetent learner, mounting and riding the unicycle with great difficulty, doing his best to look like he was made of rubber as he slid and collapsed and bounced athletically but hopelessly to everyone's loud laughter.

It was the best summer of his whole life.

And a couple of months before the summer camp, he took part in Belfast's annual Festival of Fools, a Saturday street exhibition of tumblers, stilt-walkers and clowns. Dressed in clothes too small, tight trousers that came only to his shins, a tight jacket that revealed his skinny forearms, and a painted clown face, he had romped along on a rusty old bicycle, falling off and tumbling, and generally making a fool of himself. It had been a fantastic day.

To work in a circus was his dream. He would be a clown or an aerialist, an artist of some kind one day, and he would travel around the world. He would make his home in Dublin, or some other place in the Irish Republic where there were no bombs or bullets, perhaps somewhere away out in the countryside, away from the North of Ireland and the deadly cities of Belfast and Derry—called Londonderry by Protestants. One day he would do these things, he was certain of it.

And he would work in a circus.

He might even decide to become the most famous trapeze artist in the whole world. Like Mike Ribble in *Trapeze*.

...the spit of a snake...

Thoughts of Nicole and the Youth Circus had managed to push the funeral to the back of his mind for a few minutes, and then, amazingly, after already sleeping most of the day, he slept again.

The room was dark when he woke, but then it **would** be dark, because of the painted window. It was hard to know whether it was night or day. According to his bedside clock, it was a few minutes before six AM. Breakfast was at seven. He closed his eyes. How long would he have to stay in this place? It could be a long time before the Mole was caught and sent to jail. He might be stuck here with the less-than-cheerful Grogans for weeks—months maybe. All the police had to go on was his description of the killer. Many people had moles. They couldn't round up all the mole-faced people and parade them for him to identify; it was impossible.

He felt low.

Today was Thursday, the day of the funeral.

Then there was the question: Why should he trust the police? Inspector Osborne might have no intention of catching the Mole. Why should the police try to help him, a Catholic kid—a Taig? The police worked closely with the British army soldiers to send Catholics to prison. Police and soldiers constantly stopped Catholic kids in the street to search them, insult them, beat them. "Hey! You! Yes, you dirty little Taig, get over here and stand at attention." They even searched their schoolbags. The police searched a boy from Liam's school and found him to have a knife, marker pens and glue for sniffing. They drove him up into the hills, miles from home, and dropped him off in the middle of nowhere, and he had to walk home in the rain. Everyone in the poor areas of west Belfast, Catholics and Protestants alike, despised the police. Small children, growing up under their constant contempt, name-calling and abuse, were terrified of uniforms.

Why the Prods and police called them Taigs, Liam did not know, didn't even know what the word meant. Rory the scholar said he thought the word came from an Irish word, "tadhg," an insulting nickname meaning "Irishman" or "two-faced person." All Liam knew was that if you were Catholic in west Belfast you were a Taig. He hated the word and the way it sounded in Prod mouths, like the spit of a snake.

He felt very low, like a deep black pit was waiting to swallow him up.

He couldn't let that happen. He swung himself out of bed, switched on the light, sat on the hardwood floor and started a few of the stretching exercises he'd learned at the Ballymurphy gym. He couldn't get to his regular gymnastics practices but there was no reason for not keeping himself stretched. And focused.

The ribs still hurt, restricting some of his movements, but his foot felt fine. Delia Cassidy had done a good job on it.

Half an hour later, exercises finished, he kneeled and peeped through the patch of unpainted glass. It was light outside, but it looked like the usual Belfast rain.

He made for the bathroom. The one tiny window was also painted over. He showered and looked in the mirror at his left side where his ribs hurt: black and blue, just as he'd figured. He dressed and headed downstairs for breakfast, testing his injured foot against the stair; it felt good.

Moira was in the kitchen alone. "Did you sleep?"

"Yes, thanks."

"You're a great one for the sleep, that's for sure."

She didn't say anything further until their breakfasts—fried eggs, sausages, fried potato bread (called fadge), fried potatoes—were on the table. He was hungry, so he ate everything except the fried bread. He knew his mum would pull her lemon-sucking face at so much fried stuff. Breakfast at home was usually porridge, and fruit if they could afford it. His mum said fried stuff was bad for you.

"Where's Fergus?" he asked Moira.

"Leaves for work at half-five."

"What does he do?"

"Hmmmph," was all she said.

...the larger view...

Back in his room again, he kneeled at the spy hole and looked out the window. Gray gloom. And still raining. There wasn't much to see, just an empty postage stamp of a yard and a back alley beyond. It was a long drop to the ground, and no drainpipe to swarm down in an emergency. He tried again to open the window. The wooden frame wouldn't budge. The house was old. He checked to see if the frame had been screwed shut but saw no fasteners. It was obvious from the undisturbed layers of paint that the window had not been opened in a very long time.

He did fifty push-ups on the floor, taking them slow because of his bruised ribs. Next, fifty sitting triceps dips, palms on the edge of the bed frame, feet on the floor.

Then he took a trip downstairs to the kitchen. Moira was watching the telly in the other room. He could smell her stale cigarette smoke. He grabbed a sharp, pointed potato peeler from the knife drawer, smuggled it back to his room and immediately started working on the window frame, gouging and peeling away the thick hard layers of paint between frame and casement. He needed to get the window open. Why? he asked himself. For fresh air, of course. And the work would keep his mind off today's funeral. Also, he hated the feeling of being closed in. What about escape? No: The window was much too high off the ground to risk a jump should something happen. But what could happen? It was a safe house, wasn't it?

He hadn't asked Osborne the time of the funeral—he'd said morning—but it was probably happening right now, right this very minute.

He worked away at the window for a long time, stripping away curling ribbons of paint. He had seen IRA funerals before. There would probably be two groups of six IRA men carrying the coffins on their shoulders. The potato peeler was an effective tool for the job, slicing easily under the old paint. Then there would be maybe ten or twelve uniformed and masked IRA men with guns surrounding the coffins. The paint peelings began to pile up on the floor. The British soldiers would be resting their elbows on the turrets of their armored vehicles, automatic rifles at the ready, and watching the IRA men firing their guns in the air as the coffins were lowered into the ground. Finally, after much cutting and scraping and peeling, he was able to hook his index fingers under the grips and lift the window high enough to jump out. If he wanted to. If he wanted to break his neck. And then the masked IRA men would march away, and the soldiers in the armored vehicles would continue to watch them, careful not to say anything that might start a fight. He carefully cleaned up the paint peelings and tossed them out the window. He closed the window, leaving just a crack open for fresh air. The police would be there too, sitting in their Land Rovers with binoculars and cameras with telephoto lenses. And not to forget the security forces' helicopter shooting video footage of the funeral from far above, out of the range of snipers' guns and hand-held anti-aircraft missiles. He felt satisfied about his open window. He propped himself up on his bed with pillows and went back to *Space Monsters*, but his mind was still clenched on the funeral, and he soon put the book aside.

He wasn't allowed to go outside, couldn't go to the funeral even if he wanted to.

Did Fergus leave every morning at half-five? Then this really wasn't a prison after all, was it? Not exactly what you'd call a lockdown. What was to stop him from just walking out the front door if he wanted to? Fergus had gone to work. Moira couldn't stop him, could she? An old chain-smoking lady?

But where could he go? The funeral? Where the Mole was probably waiting for him? Could he go home? The house was empty, but would the Mole or one of his fellow thugs be watching for him? And did he really want to go back there? The place where his mum and his da had been murdered? It was contaminated now by blood and horror, fear and hatred; it wasn't his home any longer.

He decided to stay where he was, for the time being anyway. He would just have to be patient; he couldn't go outside, but he could exercise and read, or he could watch the telly downstairs if he wanted. This room was quiet and private; it would suit him fine until the Mole was put away for good.

It was, after all, a safe house. He would stay.

He picked up *Space Monsters* again. After only a minute, his eyes glazed over. The book worked better than sleeping pills. It was awful. He closed his eyes and after a while found himself hovering under the ceiling, looking down on his own skinny body, sprawled on a bed in a bare room, a book in his hands. He zoomed his mind out, like a camera, pulling away higher and higher out of the room, hovering for a few seconds over the roof of the safe house, then zooming out in the pouring rain over the gleaming wet rooftops of Belfast, looking down on the domed roof of the city hall and the downtown, and row upon row of commercial buildings and houses radiating outward in every direction, and the streets, and the three motorways and the Westlink. He saw Rory and Nicole, tiny from the far distance. He zoomed out, up into the sky, and looked down on the North of Ireland. He kept moving out into space and looked down on the Irish Republic to the south, and then higher still until he could see Ireland itself as one country, without borders, surrounded by the sea, and there was Wales, the shape of a pig's head, and England too, a big boot, and now Scotland, a flying kilt, and the whole of the British Isles. He zoomed away more and more until he was hovering way out in deep space, watching the slow rotation of the planet beneath him, unable now to locate the tiny plot of earth that was Ireland.

"Isn't it splendid, Liam, up here, out of harm's way, taking the larger view of things?"

"It's brilliant, Da."

"Distance enhances the view, son, according to…"

"I miss you, Da."

"I know. But you'll be all right, son. We're remarkable proud of you, your mum and I. You're a fine boy."

Suddenly he was back in his room, lying on a bed, staring at a book.

He didn't know how long he had been staring at the book, but after a time he put it down, reached for the second book and looked at the title: *White Fang* by Jack London. There was a picture on the cover of a fierce wolf. White Fang must be the wolf's name. It was a good name for a wolf. It was not as easy to read as *Space Monsters*. The words and sentences were harder, and he had to go more slowly; any words he didn't understand he skipped, plunging on, eager to meet the wolf of the book's cover. He read of two men in the wild frozen north, Jack and Henry, with a team of six dogs and a sleigh carrying a dead man in a coffin. This was much better than space monsters. He finished the chapter. There had been no mention yet of White Fang, the wolf. But his eyes were getting too tired to read anymore. He put his book down and closed his eyes.

...arms of a child...

One of his very earliest memories is of two red ladybugs and a deafening noise. The noise comes first. Then the ladybugs.

He is a little kid walking in the street, his mum holding him by the hand. The explosion terrifies him. He clutches his mum's hand fearfully and sees on his wrist two sudden small, plump red drops that he thinks are ladybugs. He goes to touch them and sees they are splotches of blood.

What he does not remember, and so does not know, is that a bomb kills a man named Sean McCoy, a father of six, as he climbs into his car not fifty yards in front of them.

When he is eight, his mum says to his da, "What's to

stop us from leaving Belfast and sailing to England? I hear there's work for them that wants it in London. Or Birmingham or Manchester."

Liam joins in. "No way! I don't want to go to shitty England."

"I'll not have that kind of language in this house!" His mum glares at him.

"Sorry."

His da shrugs. "Well, we can't go to England, and that's that." He returns to the salad he dislikes but always eats because Liam's mum says it's good for him.

"And why not?" His mum narrows her eyes at him across the table.

"Money, for one thing. There's ferry tickets, there's lodgings…"

His mum talks fast, interrupting. "We wouldn't need much, just enough to get started. A place to stay while you find a job. You haven't had a proper job in twelve years. Bits and pieces, that's all, nothing regular. We're mad to be staying here, living hand to mouth the way we do. I could find a job too. There's plenty of work over there for women. Liam will soon be old enough to take care of himself while I work."

Liam sticks out his chest. "I can take care of myself right now."

His da finishes his salad and puts down his fork. "Chasing off to England is not the answer, darlin'. Isn't that what the Protestant Loyalists want? For us all to leave? But we'll not leave. Things will get better here now that the Good Friday Agreement is signed. Be patient. There's an old Irish saying: 'The waters wear the stones; patience is the pace of nature.'" He turns to Liam and says again, "'Patience is the pace of nature.' What d'you think of that?"

His mum winks at Liam. "Sounds more like Shakespeare to me."

His da's eyebrows disappear under his mop of hair. "And wasn't Shakespeare Irish?"

"As far as patience goes," his mum says, "haven't we been patient for over thirty years? Nothing changes. Soldiers, barely eighteen years old, not much more than children, come over here from England with their cockney accents, and search our houses whenever they feel like it, and treat us like trespassers and refugees in our own country, and shoot at us with their plastic bullets. Like poor May Furlong, only thirteen and walking home from school with her friends, and now she's a permanent basket case, in and out of hospital with a shattered mouth and jaw, one operation after another, and she'll never be the same. Shot deliberately she was. The other girls saw it."

Liam knows May Furlong. She once was a pretty girl: red hair and lovely gray eyes. Now she never goes out, unless it is dark.

His da says, "I thought we were talking about jobs."

His mum helps herself to the salad bowl. "There are no jobs."

Silence.

Liam thinks his mum's probably right about the jobs because his da puts up no argument. And she's definitely right about the way the British army treats them.

His mum thrusts the bowl at his da, "Have some more salad."

"No thanks."

"Liam?"

"No thanks."

His mum takes the bowl back and finishes the little that is left. "If there were jobs in Belfast, I'd have had one years ago. Mrs. McIntosh says…"

"Ah, don't be tellin' me about Mrs. McIntosh, Fiona darlin'. That old harridan has a tongue on her would clip a hedge. She sees only trouble and strife, that one. If she ever smiled, she'd crack herself in two."

His da gets up from the table, and Liam leaps up and throws his arms around his neck. "Da, let's never go to England, okay? We will always stay here, right?"

"Ah! No man ever wore a scarf as warm as the arms of a child," his da says, laughing and hugging Liam and whirling him around and causing his mum to leap to her feet yelling for them to stop before something gets broken.

Liam is ten:

"There's almost as many Protestants out of work as Catholics, Joe. We ought to be working together to solve our problems, not fighting each other."

Liam is standing in the street with his da and Joe Boyle, a neighbor.

Joe Boyle laughs. "You'll never see that, Daniel. Catholics and Protestants working together in the North of Ireland? You're dreaming, man, so you are."

"Don't you be so sure, Joe. That so-called Peace Line?" His da points to the twenty-foot-high brick-and-steel wall dividing the two areas, the Catholic Falls Road and the Protestant Shankill Road. "That wall should be knocked down for starters. Should have been demolished years ago. They did it in Berlin. The Berlin Wall came down, right? Well, what is stopping us from doing the same thing here? We should be opening our windows wide and shouting loud, 'I'm mad as hell and I'm not going to take it anymore!'"

"Listen to yourself talking," says Joe Boyle, shaking his head. "A dreamer you are."

"That wall divides us, Joe. How can we talk of peace if we keep a wall up between us? The Irish poet says, 'Something there is that doesn't love a wall, that wants it down.' He's right, so he is. That wall must be pulled down, Joe, before we all kill one another."

"Ah, never mind your Irish poet, Dan. You're a great one for talking. The fact is, Protestants and Catholics are like oil and water: They will never mix in a million years. The Protestants are the majority; they want to drive us out. The wall protects us. That's why we will always need the wall."

While his da and Joe are talking, Liam stares at the wall and the clouds above it and tries to imagine what he would see if it suddenly disappeared. No wall? It is hard to picture. The Peace Line wall was there long before he was born. There are streets on the other side, he knows that, streets like the one he is standing in now, streets he has never seen, with British army bases and surveillance cameras and gun towers and razor wire. Streets with police stations like forts, plump sandbags piled high around them. With houses blind with boarded-up windows to prevent Prod and Catholic terrorist firebombs. With burnt-out shops and pubs. With wire mesh, iron gratings, and metal barriers for protection. With empty lots littered with piles of rubbish and wrecked cars. With graffiti everywhere. With heavily armed police and soldiers in combat gear and visored helmets, walkie-talkies constantly crackling as they mingle with shoppers in the street, guns at the ready.

West Belfast is a war zone.

What would life be like with no wall separating the two factions? It is impossible for Liam to imagine.

...girls, wild and audacious...

He lay on his bed in the safe house, his mind teeming with thoughts and his heart crowded with feelings. Mainly he thought about his mum and his da. Sometimes he thought of Nicole.

"She's wonderful," says Nicole Easterbrook.

"Yeah, but she sure gets mad sometimes," says Grace Newton.

The four friends, Liam, Rory Cassidy, Nicole and Grace, are in the Youth Circus lounge, taking their morning break one Saturday, drinking orange juice provided by YC, and discussing Madame Dubois, the director.

Madame Dubois is in charge of everything to do with the Belfast Community Circus.

"She scares me," admits Grace. "She gave me a lecture in her office one time. Yoicks! I never want to go through that again."

Rory laughs. "You must have done something pretty bad."

"I skipped out an hour early to buy a U2 album. But I got back okay for my mother to pick me up at the usual time, so what was the big deal? Anyway, Dubois was flaming mad. Threatened to throw me out of YC." She turns to Rory. "What about you?"

"What about me what?"

"Madame Dubois. Has she ever yelled at you?"

"Of course not. I don't break rules. But if I did break a rule, she wouldn't yell at me: I'm so lovable." He grins.

The others laugh. "Anyway," Rory says to Grace, "Dubois is an old lady. You should show her some respect. She's got to be way over thirty."

"Closer to forty," says Grace. "But she looks younger. That's because she's still slim and muscular from her career as a trapeze artist."

Nicole nods. "Very fit. I've watched her work out after most of the kids have gone home. She's amazing."

Grace says, "Have you noticed that big poster in her office, the one behind her desk? Not the circus poster on the far wall. The one with the trapeze artist. That's Fay Alexander. Madame Dubois was coached by Fay Alexander. So she must have been really good."

"Who's Fay Alexander?" asks Rory.

Nicole exaggerates her amazement; her mouth drops open and her eyebrows disappear under her dark fringe. "I can't believe you never heard of Fay Alexander!"

"She was a famous trapeze artist, in America," Nicole explains. "She was the stunt flyer in a circus movie called *The Greatest Show on Earth*. It won the Oscar for Best Picture of 1952."

"Wrong year," says Grace. "*Greatest Show* was 1956."

"Who cares?" says Rory. "It's ancient history."

"Not so ancient," says Grace. "Circus artists pass their skills down to the next generation. From Fay Alexander to Madame Dubois to us. What's so ancient about that? I think it's wonderful."

"So do I," says Rory. "But that's not what I meant…"

While Rory and Grace enter into a friendly argument, Liam asks Nicole, "Do you see many movies, then?"

"Not really. Just certain ones. Like circus stories."

"Have you seen *Trapeze*? Burt Lancaster?"

Nicole nods, "I love *Trapeze*. I've seen it so many…"

Grace interrupts. "Who do you think was the technical adviser for the flying sequences in *Trapeze*?"

Rory laughs. "Not the famous Fay Alexander again!"

"You got it, smarty pants." Grace flashes him a triumphant smile.

Grace's eyes are blue, in an oval face. Her manner is often haughty. Liam has already noticed that Grace doesn't mix much with the Catholic kids. Rory is an exception; she is not so haughty when he is around.

Nicole and Grace are Protestants.

"Maybe we could watch *Trapeze* together sometime," Liam whispers to Nicole as they leave the lounge and make their way back to the circus ring.

"I would like that." Nicole's smile is warm and sincere.

"Relax," she says.

He wobbles and then topples off the slender cable, a few feet off the floor. "Yaa-aa!"

This is his umpteenth failure. "Wire walking is much harder than the balance beam," he moans.

But Nicole is enthusiastic. "You're doing fine, Liam. Keep at it, but focus more as you look ahead. Keep your knees bent and your arms higher. You're too stiff. That's it. Relax your shoulders and breathe naturally as you get your balance. Watch me."

Nicole jumps up onto the platform and walks out onto the wire, sure-footed as a watchmaker's cat, and so natural, almost like she's walking down the street. When she gets to the end of the wire she turns easily and walks back. "There. You see how easy it is?" She smiles at Liam. "Now it's your turn."

Her smile is brilliant, but even when she's not smiling, her mouth tips up at the corners. He likes the way her green eyes twinkle. Her hair is short and fine, worn just below the ears, and kind of straw-colored.

Both Nicole and Grace are a pleasure to watch when they work. They are so good, not only on the wire but also on the trampoline. One of the purposes of the trampoline is practicing aerial figures and poses for trapeze work, or flying as it is called, including dismounting and falling to the safety net. Liam is aware that it is possible to break his neck if he does not land on the net or trampoline properly. The girls are wild and audacious, sometimes putting on an exhibition of somersaults and high leaps on the trampoline without their safety harnesses that look like they will go right through the roof. They perform these jumps when the trainers, often third-or-fourth year students, are taking their break. They never jump like this if Madame Dubois is around, for she becomes angry over the slightest breach of the rules. "I do not want to tell your mothers you won't be home today because you broke your stupid little necks," she tells them. She thinks nothing of suspending kids from the program or even dismissing them from the circus entirely if the offense is serious enough.

Liam steps onto the platform, takes a deep breath and glides out along the wire once again. This time he manages to get to the halfway mark before falling.

Nicole applauds. "Good, you're improving. Just try not to be so stiff in the shoulders. Rub some more rosin on your shoes and try again."

Circus shoes, or soft-soled moccasins, allow the feet to feel the wire. The rosin helps the soles retain contact.

Again he tries, but overbalances when he is only halfway across. "I'll never make it!" He is angry with himself.

"Yes, you will," says Nicole confidently.

"I'm taking too much of your time."

"Not at all. I want to see you do this, okay?" Her patience and her brilliant smile make him so much want to please her.

This time when he walks across the wire he concentrates on relaxing his shoulders. He makes it all the way.

"Good work!" Nicole laughs. "Now turn and come back."

And he does.

He dismounts. "Great! You made it. Now it will be easier next time, and you will get better and better."

"Thanks, Nicole."

"Don't mention it."

...locks and chains...

Dinner with the Grogans: chicken, potatoes, peas. This time there was dessert, a store-bought apple pie, no ice cream.

He suddenly remembered the smuggled potato peeler. He had forgotten to slip it back into the drawer. It was still in his room. Had Moira missed it when she was preparing dinner? There was probably a spare in the knife drawer; in fact, he was almost sure he had seen an extra one there.

Otherwise dinnertime was much the same as the evening before. No conversation beyond Fergus's polite question to Liam: "Everything goin' okay?" And to Moira Grogan to pass the salt and pepper.

Retreating to his room after kitchen cleanup, Liam opened his window and looked out at the rainy landscape. He felt better with the window open, felt himself less of a prisoner. He put his hand outside, and felt the rain on his palm. The rules said he could not go outside but he could send out his hand to test the world, like Noah sending out a dove from the ark.

He closed the window, leaving a gap at the bottom, switched on the light, changed into his pajamas, and became absorbed in stretching exercises. Ribs still a bit tender. Foot okay though. It was a quiet house in a quiet area. No traffic noise here at the back of the house. After being stuck indoors for two days, the exercise relaxed him.

Exercises over, he collapsed onto his bed and reached for *White Fang*. He opened at the page where he had left off, where *White Fang* emerges from the darkness of his birth cave and sees the dazzling white world outside for the very first time. It is a second and different kind of birth for the wolf cub.

But he was unable to read: Thoughts of today's funeral kept crowding his mind. His mum and da were at this moment dead under the soil of Milltown Cemetery. They were in their coffins.

He closed his eyes and slept.

He slept for two days, Friday and Saturday and part of

Sunday, not once leaving his room, barely remembering the Grogans trying to get him to come downstairs to eat. It was like a fever, except he had no sickness, only grief.

On Sunday afternoon, he got up and showered and went downstairs. Fergus Grogan was out. Moira Grogan asked him no questions except, would he like some lunch?

He sat and ate what was put before him and soon he felt better.

After kitchen cleanup, he told Moira he wanted to telephone his friend.

"What friend?

"Rory. He lives on my street."

"Make it short."

He slid his wallet out of his hip pocket and read the number. He had never telephoned Rory before; there had never been a need. He lived right across the street, and they were in the same class. They saw each other every day at school, except for right now in the summer holidays.

Delia Cassidy answered and recognized his voice. "How are you, lovey? Are you all right? How's your foot?"

"I just called to talk to Rory."

"But you're all right, yes?"

"I'm fine, Mrs. Cassidy. Everything's fine."

"We're just back from ten o'clock Mass. I'll get him, hold on."

"Liam! Is it yourself?"

"It is. I get one call a day. This is it."

"I'm honored indeed."

"So you should be. Your mum said you just got in from Mass. So this is Sunday, am I right?"

"It's Sunday, yes." He sounded puzzled.

"Did you go to YC yesterday?"

"I did."

"Was anyone…asking for me?"

"Asking for you? No. Nobody was asking for you."

"Oh."

"Who were you thinking might be asking for you?"

"No one special. I just thought maybe…Nicole?"

"Nicole! Ah! You're right. Nicole was asking for you. I forgot."

"You're a jerk, Rory, you know that?"

Rory laughed. "I am. You're right. Sorry, Liam."

"What did she say?"

"Nothing much. Just wanted to know if you're all right."

"And what did you tell her?"

"Told her you're all right."

"You know what, Rory? Talking to you is like spitting into the wind."

He laughed. "Ma is getting a bed for you to put in my room."

"That'll be great." He made an effort to sound cheerful, like his usual self. "So long as you don't leave your stinking socks on the floor."

"Ha!" said Rory. "You should talk. Don't your own socks reek like rotten fish? Though it's not the smell so much. It's the way they make…"

"…your eyes smart," Liam finished for him. "Yes, I know, Rory. You're like a broken record."

They had used the same lines and gags on each other ever since they were little kids.

"You're so funny," said Rory. "Did I mention that everyone asks about you? You're a big hero around here: on the run from the Prod militants. You've made me famous. Like mad cow disease."

"That's enough now," shouted Moira Grogan from the kitchen.

"Tell Nicole, when you see her that I…"

"Hang up!" yelled Moira Grogan.

"Tell her I will be back soon, and…"

"You could tell her yourself by giving her a call."

"I don't have her number."

"Do you hear me, boy? I said hang up!"

"She wrote it down for you to call her. I have it here."

"Rory! You're such an idiot. Why didn't you say? Wait; I'll get a pencil and write it down." He hurried into the living room and grabbed pencil and paper. Moira Grogan looked like she was about to burst. Liam ignored her, picked up the phone again, and wrote down Nicole's number. "Okay, Rory, I have it. I gotta go."

"Take care of yourself, boyo."

"I will." He hung up the phone. It was still early in the day. It might be a good time to catch Nicole at home. He started dialing her number.

Moira Grogan came marching out of the living room, furious, a cigarette dangling from her lips. "Hang up the phone. You had your call. It's only one call a day, remember?" She reached for the telephone. Liam stopped dialing and turned his back on her. She screamed at him, "Hang up that phone right now, you hear?"

"There's another friend I have to call."

"One call a day. Don't you understand?"

"You owe me from the days I didn't come down."

She lunged for the phone. He held it away from her. She pushed him and he staggered backward. The woman was heavy and surprisingly strong. The telephone receiver fell and dangled on its cord, swinging against the wall. He stepped forward, reached down for the receiver, and accidentally pushed her. She fell to the floor with a shriek. "You struck me!"

"No I didn't." He held on to the receiver and watched her climb laboriously to her feet.

"You did. You struck me. Wait till Fergus hears about this." She retreated to the living room, crying and muttering to herself.

Old cow.

He dialed Nicole's number again.

"Hello." A woman's voice.

"Mrs. Easterbrook?"

"Yes."

"This is Liam Fogarty. I'm a friend of Nicole's from Youth Circus. Could I speak to her?"

"Yes, of course. Hold on, Liam."

"Liam? It's Nicole. It's good to hear from you."

"I can't talk long. I'm…" He couldn't think of what to say next.

Nicole said, "I gave Rory my number but wasn't sure if you could call. I'm so happy you did. It's terrible about your mum and dad—what happened, I mean. I'm sorry. I can only imagine how awful it is for you, Liam."

"Yes."

It was good to hear Nicole's voice, but her choice of words reminded him they were on opposite sides: Hers was a Protestant Loyalist family; his background was Catholic Republican (or Nationalist). Only a Protestant would say,

"I'm sorry" instead of the usual Irish Catholic, "Sorry for your trouble."

"I missed you at YC yesterday. We all did."

"Thanks. Were you flying?" Flying was the word they used for swinging trapeze work.

She gave a happy sigh. "All morning. I just love it so much. And in the afternoon Dubois taught us swinging ankle hangs. Scary! You should've seen Dubois. She's amazing. Wish you could've been there."

"Me too. But I might be a while yet."

"I know. I'm sorry. Liam?"

"What?"

"I really miss you a lot. Come back soon, okay?"

Fergus Grogan didn't return until late, after Liam had gone upstairs, so the promised tongue-lashing over the use of the telephone did not take place.

Later that night, Liam woke to the sound of footsteps on the stairs. The Grogans' bedroom door closed with a click. The digital clock showed 11:45 PM. He got up, switched off the light, closed his eyes and tried to get back to sleep. It was useless; he was wide-awake. After tossing and turning for a while, he got up, switched the light on again and leaned on the wall, stretching his back and leg muscles. Then he got back into bed and read some more of *White Fang*, hoping this would help him sleep. But it didn't work; after half an hour he gave up and let the book drop to the floor.

One o'clock. He was suddenly very hungry. Maybe this would be a good time to creep downstairs, return the potato peeler to the knife drawer and see if there was anything to eat in the fridge. He slid off the bed, turned off his light, and bare-footed it silently down the stairs.

Voices in the kitchen. Men talking quietly. Fergus and another man. The other man's voice sounded familiar. Liam tiptoed along the short hallway toward the kitchen and then stopped. Police. A uniformed constable seated at the kitchen table was speaking in a low voice to Fergus, on the opposite side of the table.

The policeman handed something, a book or an envelope, to Fergus. "You better count it," he said. "Make sure it's all there." He leaned back in his chair and took off his uniform cap.

Liam stared in horror. The Mole!

Heart and stomach plunged.

The Mole was a policeman!

Handing Fergus an envelope of money!

Why would the Mole be handing Fergus a wad of money? Liam did not know the answer, but there was one thing he did know: His life was in danger again. He had to get out of the safe house or he was dead; he had to get out now, immediately. Heart thumping wildly, he turned and moved quickly and silently back along the hallway to the front door of the house and stopped when he saw the number of locks and chains. Impossible. There was no way he could open that door without the Mole hearing him.

He crept back up the stairs to his room. His legs felt wobbly. He switched on the light, got dressed as fast as he could, and slipped the potato peeler into his pocket. Then he opened the window wide. He looked down. The window was much higher off the ground than his bedroom window at home; it was a bigger house, with higher, old-fashioned rooms. Worse, there was no drainpipe to swarm down. Any attempt to escape out the window would be crazy. How far could he run on broken legs? The Mole would catch him. No, there had to be another way. He looked around the room quickly. The bed!

Luckily the bed was close to the window. Working fast, he pulled off the sheets and blankets, knotted them together, tied one end to the leg of the bed, and threw the "rope" out the open window. It was a trick he remembered from a movie. It had worked in the movie, but would it work in real life? Movies were not real life, he knew that, but he had to try it—what else could he do? He couldn't escape from the main floor. They had it covered. He pulled on his socks and shoes and dressed himself quickly for escape. The rest of his things—a thin sweater, socks, underpants, gray wool watch cap, a couple of T-shirts—he stuffed into his backpack. Then he threw in *White Fang*. He was operating on pure nerves and instinct. He switched off the light, dropped to the floor, and rolled himself out of sight under the bed, dragging the backpack with him.

Now all he had to do was wait, heart hammering.

He did not have to wait long.

He could hear his bedroom door opening. Slowly, quietly. Then somebody switched on the light.

"Shite!"

"What the…?"

He heard the men rushing about.

The Mole's voice: "The little Taig bastard's gone out the window!"

Fergus: "Quick! He can't have got far."

The two men rushed from the room and down the stairs. He could hear them cursing and swearing as they searched for him outside.

Liam slithered quickly from under the bed, grabbed his backpack, and flew down the stairs. The front door was wide open. He could hear the men's voices outside. He ran as fast as he could out the door into the dark and the rain. He fled from the safe house, trembling and terrified, pushing his arms through the straps of his backpack as it bounced about like a wild thing on his shoulders.

...he was a maniac...

He ran through the rain, unconcerned about direction, concentrating on escape.

He heard the roar of the engine coming at him from behind. A desperate glance over his shoulder told him it was an armored police Land Rover—a "meat wagon," Catholics called it—intent on crushing his bones, cartilage, muscle, nervous system, brain, organs, and everything else that went into making the skinny parcel of humanity known to the world as Liam Fogarty. The motor thundered in his ears as it came up over the sidewalk at him. He threw himself into a doorway just in time to avoid falling under its wheels as it missed him by the width of a hand and crashed into the front door of the next house. He could see the Mole's enraged face behind the wheel, livid and contorted almost beyond recognition. The man had gone completely berserk; he was a maniac, no mistake about it. He gunned the engine and backed away from the house. Liam darted out of the doorway's protection and ran. The Mole roared after him. Legs pumping, arms whirling, Liam fled into an alleyway. The car followed, its high beam throwing Liam's own shadow eerily out in front of him. The narrow alley, not much wider than the car, left very little room for dodging. He would be creamed for sure if he didn't get back out onto the street. He was a fool to have come in, unless…with the sound of God-knows-how-many tons of speeding steel in his ears, he saw a possible way out. Leaping into the air, he grasped the wet limb of a backyard tree and hauled himself high enough for the vehicle to speed beneath him, like a bull rushing under the matador's cape. With a scream of brakes it stopped and reversed, but by then Liam had thrown his legs over the wall and dropped out of danger, temporarily, into the backyard. He picked himself up out of the mud and leaves and made a mad dash for the street. Which way now? He turned right. He got to the corner of the street and glanced back. The Land Rover was only a few hundred yards behind. There was a main road up ahead. It was Newtownards Road; he recognized Freedom Corner from the huge Prod mural, with its red hand of Ulster, painted on the wall. A city bus was just pulling in to the bus stop. He glanced back again. The Land

Rover wasn't far behind. Lungs bursting, he willed his legs to sprint for it. With a lunge he leaped onto the bus platform as the door was starting to close.

The bus driver's attention was on his mirror as he pulled out. "Trying to get yourself killed, are you lad?"

There were only a few people on the bus. He had the wallet Jack Cassidy had given him. There was one five-pound note in it. The driver did not make change; the fare was 50p. He held up the note. "I've got no change."

The driver gave him a look.

"Sorry," said Liam.

"Take a seat then."

He pushed the note back into his wallet and took a seat.

He looked back. The Land Rover was following close behind the bus, its windscreen wipers working steadily. He started brushing the worst of the dirt and leaves off his jeans and jacket. The bus crossed the River Lagan and was soon in the city center. They were slow getting through an amber light, and the Land Rover was forced to stop on the red to avoid other traffic. They pulled to a stop on the far side of the junction. This would be his best chance, while the Mole was waiting for the light. He hurled himself off the bus.

He was on Royal Avenue, not far from the Castle Court shopping center. It was after two o'clock in the morning, and he was wet, cold and tired. Mostly, though, he was scared.

He knew what would happen if the Mole caught him. The thought terrified him. He heard again the sound of guns exploding, imagined torn flesh and broken bones and his blood pooling on the wet ground.

He ran.

A twinge from his injured foot.

Where to go? Going home was no longer an option for him; he no longer had a home. Unless he counted the Cassidy place as his new home. But he couldn't go there, not now. He would have to survive on his own somehow, without endangering the Cassidy family. He couldn't depend on Osborne or the police to help him—that was now obvious. Some safe house! But it was going to be tough. The Mole was a killer. A policeman and a killer. He looked back. No sign of the Land Rover. He had no doubt that the Mole was still searching for him; he had to get off the deserted and well-lighted main road and keep to the dark lanes. He had to find a place to stay the night. And if he was going to survive, if he wasn't to end up as dead meat, then he needed time to figure out his next move.

There were seven of them—homeless men who hoarded newspapers and cardboard to help them keep warm through the night. They were behind the shopping center, in a covered loading bay lighted by a dim overhead bulb. Two appeared to be asleep, wrapped in ragged sleeping bags. The others had old bedding of different kinds, laid out on sheets of cardboard. One man turned his back on the others and swigged liquor from a secret bottle.

Liam sat a short distance from them and leaned his back against the loading bay doors. One of the men shuffled over and offered him a large cardboard box that, according to the printing on the outside, had contained a washing machine. He thanked the man, who showed him how to curl the sides of the cardboard over him and tie them together with twine. "Maytag overcoat," the man said, chuckling.

A heavy weariness penetrated through to his bones. He should be safe here for a while, he thought, and he had company for the night, unlike the scary night spent alone in the Ludlow family sepulchre. Having other people around made it seem safer. He rummaged through his backpack, found his gray wool hat and pulled it down over his head. Then he pushed himself down inside the cardboard overcoat, the dry side of his backpack under his head, closed his eyes and, in spite of his damp jeans, dropped into an uneasy sleep.

...everyone has his price...

He woke with a start. A filthy bearded rat of a man, smelling as if he had just crawled out of the sewer, was kneeling beside him, stroking his head and murmuring words in his ear. Terrified, he sat up quickly and kicked out with his feet. "Get off!"

The man fell backward onto his behind and scrambled away on all fours.

Liam tried to get back to sleep but it was useless. He was too cold and damp. And it wasn't so safe here after all. He lay in the darkness, eyes wide open, waiting for the daylight.

His mind went back over his incredibly narrow escape from the so-called safe house. The Mole had almost got him. If he hadn't crept downstairs to satisfy his hunger, he would be dead by now for sure, with a bullet through his head or a knife through his heart. Which reminded him that he was still hungry. And that Grogan! Taking a bribe! Judas! The Mole, being a policeman, must have found a way to discover the address of the safe house and make Grogan an offer he couldn't refuse. Trustworthy: That was the word Inspector Osborne had used for Grogan and his wife. And Catholics too!

Everyone had his price.

Liam and his da are walking together along the street on their way to a football match. It's Sunday, it's sunny, and the Ballymurphy Warriors are playing the Boxhill Centurions.

A man approaches. He opens his dirty raincoat. Liam stares. There are dozens of watches attached to the man's coat. "I got digitals and regulars," the man says. "I got real silver pocket tickers, and I got ladies' cocktail…"

"No thanks," says Dan Fogarty, pushing past the man.

"Real cheap," says the man. "Digitals for only…"

"No thanks," says Dan Fogarty again, walking on.

The man shrugs and goes away.

"Stolen, most likely," says Liam's da. "We will have no dealings with a thief."

Liam says nothing. He has never owned a watch. It would be good to have a watch. The watches were cheap. Why not buy one if you have the cash?

"Always be a man," says his da. "A man sticks to his principles; he does what is right. Sometimes it's a temptation to tell a lie, or steal, or cheat, or buy stolen property because it's cheap, or any number of things. People will try to persuade you to do something you know is wrong. They will try to buy you with money, or promise you fame or favor. Some would sell their souls for a bottle of wine. They say that everyone has his price. They say that everyone can be bought. Well, don't you believe it, son. Make yourself strong so no one can buy you. Maintain strong principles. That's what it means to be a man." He grinned and tousled Liam's hair. "You understand?"

"I think so."

"The Irish poet says it best: 'There's no need to fear the wind if your stack of hay is well tied.'"

"Stack of hay?"

"Your principles, son. Your beliefs."

"Heavy stuff, Da."

"I know, Liam. But my job is to love you and take care of you and help you become the best man you can possibly be."

It looked like the Mole had found Fergus Grogan's price, right enough.

But why would the Mole need to bribe Grogan when all he needed to do was attack the safe house the same way he and his partner had attacked Liam's house to kill his mum and his da? Attack and kill, wasn't that the Mole's way? So maybe it was Grogan, after all, who had contacted the Mole. Or maybe it was Protestant Inspector Osborne who set the Mole onto him. Liam gave up: He would never figure it out; he would never know. But Grogan was a traitor, that was for sure, and a murderer—no better than the Mole.

He thought about what Delia Cassidy had said about the IRA killing the people in Omagh. Catholics were supposed to be the good guys, weren't they? The saints and heroes. Ireland, the home of the brave. He had grown up with his friends believing the Prods were the bad guys. One thing Liam understood was that his da was right: There was good and bad on both sides. The Prods he had met at the circus were good guys. Catholic Grogan was a bad guy. And the Catholic IRA people who exploded the Omagh bomb, killing twenty-nine, not counting the unborn twins, and crippling about three hundred others, were also bad guys.

The Mole was a Prod. A very bad guy. Liam had to get the Mole before the Mole got him. But how? Should he call Inspector Osborne and tell him the Mole was a policeman—one of his own men? And that Grogan was not to be trusted? But what if Inspector Osborne was one of the bad guys too? It was Osborne who had sent him to the safe house wasn't it? And what about the police driver who had taken him to the safe house? Probably a Prod.

Maybe they were all in it together. Who could be trusted?

A shivering started in his shoulders and moved to his jaw and teeth. He crawled out of his Maytag overcoat, grabbed his backpack, and hurried off into a thin drizzle of rain. Where could he go? If only he could get out of the city to a place where the Mole would not find him. Maybe he could smuggle himself onto an Ulsterbus. It wouldn't matter which town. He headed for the bus station, keeping away from open areas where the Mole might spot him, certain that the Land Rover couldn't be very far away.

...violent protests in Ardoyne...

He hunkered down in the deserted bus station. The rain had stopped. Soon it would be daylight.

Maybe he should go to the police for protection once again, to Inspector Osborne. He had seemed okay when they talked in his office, seemed genuinely concerned about his safety. But now that Liam knew the Mole was a policeman...But then again...And what if...

He felt drowsy. He tried to figure out how to board a bus—one leaving for the south of Ireland, preferably Dublin—anywhere far from Belfast where the Mole could not find him. The five pounds in his wallet would not be enough to buy a ticket. He would have to smuggle himself onto the bus. He was scared that the Mole would find him first.

He had spent a large part of his life being scared.

He remembered how scared he was going to school when he was six, and the family lived in north Belfast. At that time, there were violent protests in Ardoyne, a Protestant area. Catholics—mothers and their small children—had always passed through the Protestant estate to get to the Holy Cross Catholic Primary School, but now the Protestants wanted it to stop. "Stay out of our neighborhood!" they yelled.

Liam's mum escorted him to and from the school every day. The protests grew angrier, becoming so loud and violent that the Catholic women and children came to depend on the protection of a security forces bodyguard—army and police— carrying shields and wearing black riot gear as they acted as a buffer between the Catholics and the Protestant protesters.

"Hold my hand tight," his mum says as they join the other Catholic women and children and begin walking toward Holy Cross School.

The angry Protestants stand outside their houses, waiting. When the Catholics and their bodyguard approach the houses, the Protestant women begin screaming, blowing whistles, hooting air horns, banging bin lids on the pavement.

The din is frightful.

Some of the Protestant children begin throwing stones at the Catholics. Their parents do nothing to stop them.

The security forces bodyguard does its best to protect the Catholic children with their shields.

"Don't be scared," Liam's mum says. "And don't look at them. Keep your eyes fixed straight ahead. Be brave."

But he isn't brave; he is scared. This early-morning torture has been going on too long. He cannot understand why the Prods are so angry. His mum tried to explain it to him before they set out, on their first day. "It's a Protestant loyalist area," she told him. "But Catholics have always used this route to the school. It's too far to go around the other way. Suddenly the Prods have decided we can't walk through their streets any longer. But we have a right to walk wherever we wish. We can't let them see we're afraid."

They walk on. The din becomes louder. His mum gives a cry. A stone has hit her on the face. Liam can see the blood leap to her cheek, but she doesn't stop, just holds his hand tighter and marches on with the other women and children through the gauntlet of hate.

His mum and his da discuss it later that evening.

His mum says, "Four Catholic women found death threats in their mailboxes. Just for taking their children to school through their street! The Protestants have all gone mad. Death threats! And attacking wee children on their way to school! What next, I wonder? Yesterday, someone threw a blast bomb at the police escort. The noise was deafening. The Catholic women pushed their children to the ground and covered them with their bodies, thinking they were about to be killed. The wee children were crying and screaming with fright."

Liam sticks out his chest proudly. "I didn't cry or scream."

"I'll come with you tomorrow," his da says. "Liam can walk between us."

His mum says, "And you should hear the horns and whistles! And the bin lids banging on the pavement."

"The bin lids are plastic nowadays," his da says as he gently washes his mum's swollen cheek with alcohol and affixes a Band-Aid. "Those Protestant women today were imitating the old 'hen patrols' of the seventies, when Catholic women drummed their metal bin lids on the pavements to warn of police and army soldiers in the neighborhood. Do you remember? I was only a wee lad myself, but I remember the noise could be heard for miles around. I'm unlikely ever to forget those jungle drums. It was wild. 'Louder than the clang of a thousand trumpets,' wrote the great Irish poet Hughie Houlihan. There now! How does that feel?" He stands back.

Liam's mum touches her swollen cheek with her fingertips.

His da kisses the top of her head. "You're a brave and lovely-looking woman, sure enough."

"Ah, go on with you," says his mum, trying not to smile.

Liam was only six. But he remembered it very well. He also remembered a time later when he was eight; they had moved to Ballymurphy, and he is asking his da about grandparents.

"Is this my grandma and my granddad?"

He is frowning over a framed photograph on the chest of drawers in his mum and da's room. His da is trying to take an afternoon nap. His mum is downstairs working in the kitchen.

His da opens one eye. "It is," he says.

"They're the da and mum of you, isn't that right, Da?"

"No, not me, son. They're the mum and da of your mum. That's who they are. They're your mother's parents. Which means they are your grandparents."

"Where are they? Why don't they come to see me?"

"Ah, they're both gone, Liam darlin'. Your grandmam, God rest her soul, died of a fever many years ago. And your granddad didn't last long after that, may they rest in peace."

"Granddad is a very tall man in the picture. I can't see the top of his hat."

"He was a tall man right enough."

"Where's the picture of the da and mum of you then, Da?"

"There isn't one. I grew up in foster homes."

"What's foster homes?"

"Places where people take care of kids who have no mum and da to take care of them."

Liam puzzles over this for a long time. Then he asks, "Didn't you have a mum and da, Da?"

"No, son, I didn't."

He puzzles even longer over this, still staring at the picture in its metal frame.

His da says, "I'm taking a nap now, son."

"Da?"

"What?"

"My granddad was tall. Does that mean I'll be tall too?"

"There's an old Irish saying, son: You've got to do your own growing, no matter how tall your granddad was."

Silence as Liam thinks this over. Then: "Da, you never go to church like me and Mum. Does that mean you've got no religion?"

"When you do good you feel good; when you do bad you feel bad. That's all the religion your father ever needed. I learned that from a famous Irishman named Abraham Lincoln. Now buzz off and let me take a nap."

And later, when he is ten:

"'An eye for an eye makes the whole world blind.'"

"Another old Irish saying, Da?"

"It is."

They are starting their dinner.

"Say grace, please Liam," says his mum.

"For what we are about to receive may the Lord make us truly grateful."

"Good boy. Help yourselves to the veggies." His mum passes him a bowl.

Liam digs in. "What does it mean?" He passes the veggies to his da.

His da takes the bowl. "What does what mean?"

"That eye stuff."

His da says, "It's in the Bible. And the Koran. Eye for eye, tooth for tooth, life for life. It means you strike back if someone strikes you. It means if a man takes a life then he must lose a life. Vengeance. Revenge. You understand?"

"I think so. Except the blind part. What is it again?"

"'An eye for an eye makes the whole world blind.' Mahatma Gandhi said it. What do you think he meant?"

"I thought you said it was an old Irish saying."

His da's thick black eyebrows disappear for a moment under his mop of hair. "Mahatma Gandhi was Irish—everyone knows that. His real name before he ended up in India was Mickey Gannon, from County Clare."

Liam thinks for a few seconds, and then he says, "I give up. I don't know what he meant."

"Think about it while you're dribbling your dinner down the front of your sweater."

His mum cries, "Oh, Liam. That's your new school sweater. You're supposed to take it off when you get home! What have I told you?"

Liam dabs gravy off his sweater. "Sorry. I forgot."

His mum sighs. "What are you two going on about anyway?"

His da nods toward the newspaper. "Story about a young eighteen-year-old man stabbed to death by a nineteen-year-old man. Both of them Protestants. Pictures on the front page. Liam was asking why a Protestant would kill another Protestant. The police think it's a feud between two gangs."

His mum says, "They're killing each other? Is that it?"

His da shrugs. "Gang warfare. Crime, drugs, who knows?" He turns to Liam. "Did you figure it out, the meaning of 'An eye for an eye makes the whole world blind'?"

"Revenge is a bad idea? Everyone loses?"

"Good lad." His da ruffles Liam's hair.

Liam grins at his mum. His mum winks back at him.

...runaway boy...

Daylight. Rain and wind. Summertime in Belfast. He peered out the dirty windows of the cold and drafty bus depot. Glengall Street was deserted. He turned away from the windows and sat huddled on one of the wooden benches and waited.

After a while, the ticket booth opened its shutters. A couple of people were waiting, a man and a woman.

He got to his feet and walked up and down, reading the place names on the buses in the depot as they waited to begin their journeys: Omagh, Londonderry, Dungannon, Enniskillen, Dublin. Just names to him. What would it be like to see different places? If he lived in Dublin, the Mole would never find him. He could get a job, change his name, dye his hair, travel around Ireland. But what about the two killers. They would go free. He hated them. He wanted them punished; he wanted them sent to rot in jail for the rest of their lives. He wanted revenge.

An eye for an eye makes the whole world blind.

His da believed it. He loved his da. Could his da be wrong? Could Mickey Gannon of County Clare be wrong?

The coffee shop opened. He thought about food. But no; he might need his money later. People were starting to arrive at the bus station.

He watched as a woman dragged a small boy along behind her to the ticket office. The child was crying. "I told you to stay with me," barked the woman. "Someone will snatch you away and then I will never have you anymore. And you will never have me." This made the child cry even louder.

He had checked the timetable. The Dublin bus was due to leave at a quarter past eight. He looked up at the clock: 7:45. The driver of the blue Ulsterbus express to Dublin arrived, climbed up onto his bus and left his raincoat beside his seat. Then he hopped down again and headed over to the coffee shop to join two other drivers seated at a table.

Liam looked out the windows again. By now the wet street was busy with traffic.

Suddenly—a police Land Rover!

He stepped back from the window. It was the Mole, he was sure of it, slowly cruising the street, searching for him.

Had the Mole seen him before he stepped away from the window?

The door of the Dublin bus was open. No one was looking. His gray wool cap pulled down low over his head, he stepped quickly onto the empty bus and sat on the floor at the back, behind a seat, where he hoped nobody would see him. He pushed his backpack under the seat and waited anxiously. If the driver saw him, then he was finished.

After a while, when there was a small crowd of people lining up outside the bus, the driver slid into his seat behind the wheel and began punching their tickets. A plump woman sat at the back of the bus, close to Liam's hiding spot. She gave him an angry look. He ignored her.

When everyone was aboard, the driver started the engine. So far, the only one who had noticed Liam sitting on the floor at the back of the bus was the plump woman. She was well dressed in a brown coat and hat, with a large handbag and brown gloves. Liam couldn't wait for the bus to get rolling and on its way. His stomach swooped with anxiety. What was holding the driver up? Go, go!

It was possible that the Mole had seen him waiting in the station; there were very few people about, and the Land Rover had been moving slowly enough for the Mole to spot him.

The bus started moving. Liam breathed a sigh of relief. He leaned back and closed his eyes. He was going to make it.

The bus stopped. What now? He heard the door opening. Pause. A voice: "Anyone seen a runaway boy? He was in the bus station a few minutes ago."

The Mole!

What lousy luck. His heart plunged.

The plump woman yelled, "Back here! He's sitting on the floor."

He was done for. He was as good as dead. The Mole had him. He peeped out from behind the seat. The Mole, larger than life, in uniform, making for him, lunging down the aisle with his big shoulders and dead eyes.

Then the big arm was around his neck, cutting off his air. He felt himself hoisted easily off the floor. His wool cap fell to the floor. The Mole hauled him effortlessly to the front of the bus. Liam managed to slide his hand into his hip pocket and grasp the potato peeler. The Mole dragged him down the steps of the bus and out the door. Liam could not breathe. Gripping his potato peeler firmly, he plunged it into the Mole's thigh. The Mole groaned with pain, released his hold, and Liam fell to the ground. The potato peeler skittered away. Liam gulped air into his tortured lungs. The Mole reached down, grabbed him again, hauled him across the parking lot to the Land Rover, tossed him like a sack of laundry into the backseat and slammed the door shut.

...trapped...

It took a while for him to recover his breath while grenades exploded in his lungs. His windpipe felt crushed. The Mole was behind the wheel, and the Land Rover was speeding away from the bus depot. He checked the doors, searching for a handle, but the rear-door handles had been removed. He was trapped.

His feet became entangled in something on the floor. He bent down and pulled it away. It was a traveling rug. He picked it up off the floor and threw it onto the seat beside him.

Was this it, then? Was this the end—the Mole taking a witness who knew too much to some deserted place to kill him and then toss his corpse into a rubbish tip?

The anger boiled up in him. "You killed my mum and da!" he screamed at the back of the Mole's head. "And now you want to kill me!"

"Shut up you grubby little Taig!" growled the Mole, adding several swear words. "You're gonna be real sorry for sticking me. I'm gonna make you suffer for that—wait and see." He removed his uniform cap and tossed it onto the seat beside him. Then he popped several pills from the palm of his hand into his open mouth and swallowed them.

Liam peered beyond the bouncing windscreen wipers and saw that they were near Donegall Square. He could see the domed top of the city hall up ahead.

He was about to be tortured, by the sound of it, and then he would be killed.

But not without a fight.

They were now speeding along May Street, not far from the intersection with Oxford Street.

The light was green. He was desperate. It seemed to him that sometimes you only got one chance and if you didn't take it…It was now or never, like reaching for the swinging trapeze. Only a split second to act. If you missed the bar you dropped like a stone to the ring floor, or to the catch net, and broke your legs. Or, worse, your neck. He had already snatched the rug from the seat beside him and was now spreading it out between his hands. He reached forward over the seat and quickly threw the rug over the Mole's head, winding it tightly round his neck and jerking it back, hard and fast. The rug covered the Mole's eyes and mouth, blinding him and cutting off his air. Liam held on with all his strength, pulling the Mole's head back hard against the headrest.

Muffled yells. The Mole thrashed about and slammed his foot hard on the brake. Liam was thrown forward and into the front of the Land Rover. His head struck the dashboard. The car skidded out of its lane, collided into the car beside it with a scream of metal and plastic, and careened on, skidding and fishtailing wildly before walloping the side of a second car hard and coming to an abrupt stop. The Mole's rug-covered head slammed into the steering wheel. Liam was tossed about like a ping-pong ball. Adrenalin pumping through every vein and artery, he quickly recovered, shoved frantically at the front door handle, threw his weight against the door and fell out into the debris-strewn intersection.

He clambered to his feet and did not waste time looking to see if the Mole was following as he ran shakily into St. George's Market. He fled through the shoppers and the aisles of fish, fruit and vegetables.

But the Mole wasn't far behind; Liam could hear him yelling, "Stop that boy!"

He glanced over his shoulder. The Mole, wearing his uniform cap and running with a limp, was chasing him. Liam kept going, pushing his way through the crowd.

"Stop him! Stop that boy!"

A dutiful, law-abiding fruit vendor reached out toward Liam, trying to catch him. Liam dodged around him and ran, pausing only to pull over the man's cart full of watermelons. The melons crashed to the ground and bounced about. The Mole fell and crawled about on hands and knees amid a green sea of melons. Liam ran on, darting around a fishmonger and upsetting his display of fish, filling the aisle with halibut, haddock, cod, skate and skittering pellets of ice. Liam skidded on ice and fell forward into the stall. Behind him the Mole slipped on ice and fell again, this time onto his back. Liam scrambled to his feet as several shoppers moved in. They tried to grab him, but he dodged, turned and ran. He looked back; two stout fishmongers in white-striped blue aprons were helping the Mole to his feet.

Liam ran on. His head hurt. He felt with his fingers as he ran. There was a swelling on his right temple from his collision with the dashboard. He made for the market's Oxford Street exit. Now what? He didn't know. Find a place to hide? That would be difficult; the Mole, in spite of his thigh wound, was close on his heels.

He ran through the market looking for the exit. He was scared. Terrified, more like. He wanted to kill the Mole. He wanted to kill him slowly, wanted to make him suffer.

An eye for an eye makes the whole world blind.

He was now outside, on Oxford Street. The rain had stopped.

The fearful sound of Lambeg drums—like a dozen jet planes breaking the sound barrier—made him realize that today was July twelfth and the annual Orange Day Parade. He saw the marchers, hundreds of them on May Street, heading toward city hall with their flutes, bagpipes, accordions, trombones and kettledrums. The thunder of the giant Lambegs could be heard all over the city. People turned out in their thousands to watch the parade. There were dozens of banners and flags, paper Union Jacks and orange balloons. It was the marching season, and all over the North of Ireland the Orange Parade was taking to the streets to celebrate the victorious 1690 Battle of the Boyne, and the Protestant Loyalist ties with England. The Orange Lodge men wore dark suits, black bowler hats, white gloves, and orange sashes; other marchers wore a mix of orange lilies, orange shirts, orange jackets, orange ties, orange vests, or orange armbands. Some of the marchers threw orange-wrapped toffees to the eager children on the sidewalk.

Liam raced down Oxford Street into May Street. He looked back. The Mole was just emerging from the market but hadn't yet spotted him. Liam snatched an orange paper hat from an unresisting bystander's head and ran into the middle of the marchers. He pulled the hat down low over his ears to hide his long dark-brown hair and moved gradually through the parade, away from the Mole.

He looked back. The Mole was holding his thigh with one hand and limping quickly along the sidewalk, searching for him among the marchers. He had guessed that Liam might join the parade. Liam kept his head turned away. If he left the parade and attempted to find a hiding place, the Mole would see him for sure. It was better to keep making his way forward through the marchers and watch for an opportunity to disappear.

But he saw no opportunities.

The march eventually brought the parade to the city hall, where it stopped. He kept moving, leaving the marchers and hurrying across to the Linenhall Street entrance of city hall. It was a mistake: He should have stayed with the parade. When he looked back, he could see that the Mole had spotted him.

He ran into the city hall. A large group of tourists stood between the marble statues in the ornate entrance hall, blocking his way. He pushed through into the center of the tourists and hid among them like a bird in a cornfield. His right temple hurt. He felt the spot with his fingers, checking for blood, but there was none, only the swelling. He let his orange hat drop to the floor.

"It's a copy of the dome on St. Paul's cathedral in London," the guide, a thin, bushy-haired, university student, was saying as he pointed up to the roof.

Liam, peeping out from his hiding place, saw the Mole arrive and stare about him wildly, his face streaked with traces of blood, probably from the car crash. He limped to the staircase, searching for Liam, and looked up toward the gallery. Then he hurried back to the tourist group and started pushing his way through them. "Stand aside!" he yelled.

Liam could almost smell the hatred and violence burning out of him.

The Mole had committed a double murder. A boy had seen him do it. The boy also knew he was a member of the Ulster Constabulary. He had to silence that boy. The only way to silence that boy was to kill him. It was as simple as that.

As the Mole moved, so did Liam, keeping a distance between them. The Mole began to move more aggressively, shouldering people aside. Voices were raised. A woman screamed. Somebody fell to the marble floor. A man yelled. Another woman screamed. The Mole had seen him and was struggling to reach him, knocking to the floor an old woman with a cane. "Hold that boy!" yelled the Mole.

Liam fled the group before anyone could hold him and ran two steps at a time up wide marble staircases: one flight, two flights, three flights, four flights. He stopped and leaned on the banister to look down at the flights below. The Mole, not as quick as Liam, was several flights down. Liam could see the top of his head as he grasped the banister and pushed himself to catch up, dragging his injured leg up the steps. Considering that he was wounded, the Mole was moving remarkably fast.

Liam continued moving up the steps. Where did they lead? Was he running into a dead end where the Mole could catch him? Maybe he would have been better off staying out on the open streets and making a run for it. Or maybe he should have stayed with the tourists. Would someone have protected him? Probably not. Who would interfere in a police chase, except to aid the police? Besides, how could any of them have stood up against such a big angry man in a police uniform?

...sound of the circus...

Angry man.

Liam is eight. He kicks his soccer ball—a homemade wrap of used car tire and rags—through the window of the house next door, breaking several panes of glass. The ball bounces onto the kitchen table and upsets Mr. Tiernan's mug of freshly brewed tea. The tea spills onto Mr. Tiernan's hand and scalds him.

Neighbor Jack Tiernan, new on the street, is "not quite right in the head," according to local gossip. His reputation for strange and unorthodox behavior is tested. He comes roaring over the backyard wall like a demented lion (Liam's da tells Fiona Fogarty later), grabs Liam by the shoulders, and shakes him until teeth and tonsils rattle.

Liam's da sees what is going on and rushes out to rescue his son. Tiernan will not let Liam go. He is like a bulldog with his teeth clenched on enemy flesh. Dan Fogarty bops Tiernan lightly on the nose. Tiernan stops shaking Liam and clasps his nose. Surprised, he whirls about to face his attacker. Liam's da smiles, puts his arm round Tiernan's shoulders and talks to the man in a gentle voice, at the same time leading him back through the yard gate to his own place.

"I didn't enjoy causing the poor man pain," Dan Fogarty tells Liam and his mother afterward, "but I had to act fast before he shook the life out of the lad. The man lost his temper. Maybe it's a good thing it happened; now we're the best of friends."

"The guy's crazy," says Liam. "I thought he'd kill me."

"'The soft answer turns away wrath,' says the Irish poet."

"Thumping the man on the nose was hardly a soft answer," says Liam's mum. "Was it bleeding?"

"Not a bit," says Dan Fogarty indignantly. "It was a soft answer of a blow."

His da had protected him then. He needed his da, now, to protect him from the Mole. Perhaps he was protecting Liam from his new place up in Heaven, lending strength to his legs, helping him think of ways to escape.

Liam looked back. The Mole was coming after him. He was unstoppable. Liam plunged up a final staircase to the top and then ran to the end of a gallery, to a tight corridor that ended with a door in front and doors to the sides. He pushed through the door in front of him and hurried inside. The door had a lock. He clicked it on; the lock gave back a reassuring sound of temporary safety. He turned and leaned his back against the door while he recovered his breath. The door was thick and solid. To get through it the Mole would have to get security to open it with a key.

Time to think.

The Mole was on the other side of the door. Liam could hear him try the lock and push at the door with his shoulder. Then he tried to kick the door open, but both door and lock were too strong for him.

Silence.

He had gone away. How long would it take him to find someone with a key?

He had to get out of the room.

But where to run?

At the far end of the room, there was a short flight of metal steps with handrails leading up to narrow metal doors that opened outward like shutters on the outside of the dome. The doors were open. He climbed the steps and found himself looking through the open doors at a cloudy sky. He leaned out the doors cautiously and looked down at a narrow granite parapet, no wider than a foot, that ran around the bottom of the city hall's dome like the very narrow brim of a bishop's hat. From where Liam stood, it was a sheer drop to the ground of two trapeze heights, or eighty feet. There were ropes. Slung twenty or twenty-five feet below the parapet were two window cleaners' platforms with a man on each platform, washing windows. This explained why the metal doors were open.

He could not go back. The Mole would soon be bursting into the room. Either Liam could swarm down one of the window cleaners' ropes, ending up on one of their platforms, or he could move forward onto the granite parapet and attempt an escape by climbing down a drainpipe to the ground. Then he saw another possible way. About ten yards up ahead, on the outside of the dome, was another opening, similar to the one where he now stood, its double metal doors opened out onto the side of the dome like a pair of shutters. He rejected the idea of swarming down the rope to what would certainly be an easy place for the Mole to shoot him. Instead he could walk along the parapet to the next opening and dodge back into the building and hide somewhere or get back down to the street. That is, if he could walk along the parapet, one foot in front of the other in circus wire-walking fashion, without falling to what would be certain death below.

He could hear someone at the door behind him. The lock clicked and tumbled as a key released the bolt. He was seconds away from being caught, dragged away and executed.

He had no choice. He stepped out onto the parapet and stood, finding his balance. He took a deep breath and began moving slowly, away from the opening, balancing himself, hands at waist level, shoulders relaxed, the way Nicole had taught him, stepping out as though on the high wire at the circus or the balance beam at the gym. The rain had stayed off. The parapet was dry. There was very little wind. He did not look down at the ground far below but kept his gaze fixed on the way ahead, to the next opening. Though only about ten yards away, it seemed like a mile. He imagined himself high above the circus ring, walking the tight wire. He imagined the sound of the circus crowd below as it sucked in its collective breath and waited in agonized anticipation. Sweat broke out on his forehead. His head throbbed. He had forgotten about the swelling at his temple. Circus spectators had no idea how much an aerialist suffers if he is unwell on the day of the performance, he thought. One step at a time; one foot in front of the other. Lightly, carefully. He imagined Nicole encouraging him: "That's it, Liam. Keep going."

Hc was almost there. Nicole's happy face. Relax. Take it easy. No hurry.

An imaginary roar of appreciation from the crowd below told him he had reached the metal door. He held on with both hands, swallowing with relief.

He turned and faced back the way he had come, expecting to see the Mole glaring out at him from the other door, but there was no sign of him. Perhaps he had gone back inside, planning to catch him with the help of a security guard at this second open door. But no! The Mole now stuck his head out the far door, saw Liam, and started to climb out onto the parapet!

Liam stared. The man was mad. Rage had made him blind. Mole blind. So intent was he on killing Liam, that he seemed unaware of the danger. Liam left the parapet, stepping through the door into a room similar to the first. Now that his feet were on safe ground, he was able to lean out the door and look back at his pursuer. He decided to wait. If the Mole was foolish enough to walk the parapet and managed to make it to Liam's door, Liam could easily push him off without any danger to himself and that would be the end of the Mole.

The Mole crawled out of his door onto the parapet, breathing heavily, red-faced, eyes staring madly. He tried to stand on the parapet but failed. He sank to his knees and began crawling slowly along the parapet toward Liam's door. He crawled only a few yards before he stopped, scared, as if suddenly realizing his predicament. He tried to change his mind and move back but almost fell. He clutched the stone parapet desperately. "Help!" he yelled down to the window cleaners. "Help!"

The window cleaners looked up. "Hold it there!" one of them yelled.

"Hang on!" yelled the other as he switched on the electric motor that raised and lowered the platform. The platform began moving upward, like a slow elevator, until it was level with the parapet and then it stopped. But the Mole was several feet away from the safety of the platform. The window cleaner stretched out his arms but could not quite reach him. He was wearing a safety harness. He tied one end of a rope to his platform, climbed onto the parapet, and started crawling toward the Mole with the rope. "Tie the rope round your chest!" he yelled. The Mole, his back toward the window cleaner, reached back for the rope, slipped, swayed, tried to recover but overbalanced and fell, plunging into space, arms fluttering like the wings of some great black bird, bouncing off the second window cleaner's platform and plummeting to the ground, screaming like the wind.

...a great black bird...

By the time Liam had controlled his trembling enough to climb back down through the gallery and descend the marble staircase to the outside pavement, a crowd had gathered.

Liam pushed his way to the front. The Mole lay on his back, perfectly still, arms outstretched, eyes closed. A man and a woman were crouched beside him. The woman searched for the Mole's neck pulse. An ambulance arrived. Two ambulance men exchanged a few words with the man and woman as they examined the Mole. They moved him onto a stretcher, tucked a blanket around him, and then loaded the stretcher into the ambulance and drove away.

Liam discovered that he was shivering, whether from fear or from the cold he didn't know. And his head ached. The small crowd broke up as the spectators moved off.

Was the Mole still alive? It looked like maybe he was. On the telly, didn't they always cover the face if the person was dead? The ambulance men hadn't covered the Mole's face. But Liam needed to know for sure. He headed for the nearby hospital, running to warm himself up. The rain started. By the time he got to the hospital, he was quite wet. The woman on the information desk gave him change for the telephone.

He dialed the number.

It was ringing.

"Hello?"

"Mrs. Cassidy—Delia—it's me, Liam. I'm at the hospital. The Mole—he's had an accident."

"What! What are you saying?"

"The man who was trying to kill me. He fell. He's here in the hospital. Could you tell Jack—Mr. Cassidy? And could you call the police—Inspector Osborne?"

"Liam! Where exactly are you? Are you in Emergency? Which hospital?"

"Royal Victoria. Information desk."

"Jack will call Osborne. Stay right where you are. We will be there, quick as we can."

He paced the entrance lobby. The Information woman told him he could sit in the waiting room. She pointed. He opened the door and looked in; sad faces looked up at him. He closed the door, turned away and resumed his pacing, thinking about the Mole, seeing him falling like a stone.

…makes the whole world blind…

The Cassidys were the first to arrive, bursting through the swing doors, straight to where he was waiting. They had taken a taxi.

"Liam! You're all right?" Delia Cassidy sounded like his mother. Her worried gray eyes quickly took in his appearance, noticing everything about him, especially the lump on his temple and his wet, scruffy appearance. She came close and examined the bruise. She smelled good. It was like being close to his mother. Mum always smelled good—soap, fresh-baked bread…He missed her something terrible.

He shrugged. He couldn't speak. Thoughts of his mother made him a mute.

Rory said, "Hey, boyo."

Jack Cassidy said, "What happened?"

Delia Cassidy put her arm around Liam's shoulders, led him to a bench and sat him down beside her. She pushed back his hair and examined the bruise on his temple more thoroughly. "We should never have trusted Osborne. I knew something would happen. I said to Jack, I said…"

"What are you doing here, boy? Why aren't you at the safe house?" It was Inspector Osborne, uniformed and angry.

Liam glared at him. He was no longer intimidated by the man and his uniform. "They tried to kill me."

Delia Cassidy clasped his shoulders, as though to protect him from the policeman.

Osborne frowned. "Who tried to kill you?"

Liam felt a terrible tiredness and wanted to lie down. He had to force himself to speak. "Grogan and the man with the mole. He's a police officer. One of your men. Gave Grogan money. They tried to kill me. I escaped. He's here—the man with the mole is here, the policeman. In the hospital. He fell off…city hall…dead, I think."

"When? How long ago was he brought in?"

"Ambulance…just now."

"What about Grogan? Where is he?"

Liam shrugged. "At the house…"

Delia Cassidy sat up straight, shoulders back, steely gray eyes, cold stare. "So much for the protection of our city police, yes, Inspector? What kind of a safe house is it that wants to murder a young defenseless boy?"

The inspector silently fingered his ginger mustache. Then he said, "Please wait here." He strode away toward the information desk.

Delia Cassidy said, "Where is your backpack, Liam?"

"On an Ulsterbus. In Dublin by now."

"Never mind." She sighed, rolling her eyes at her husband. "I would like to give that self-satisfied police inspector a kick up the behind, so I would."

Jack Cassidy shrugged. Rory sat beside his mother and Liam. "Here, have a Mint Imperial," he said to Liam.

"Thanks." Liam took one from the bag. It had no taste.

The hospital was busy. Liam watched a bent old man shuffling along the corridor, pushing a wheeled medicine bottle contraption ahead of him. He stopped for several seconds to catch his breath and then shuffled on. Liam felt like that old man: worn out, powerless.

The inspector came back. His blue eyes looked weary. To Liam he said, "The Mole, as you call him, might survive. Or he might not. It's too soon to know. I would like to ask you a few more questions."

"We are taking Liam home," said Delia Cassidy haughtily. "There will be time for questions tomorrow. Not today. Can't you see the boy is half dead?"

"My wife is right, Inspector," said Jack Cassidy. "Your questions will have to wait."

"Very well," said the inspector. He said to Liam, "I will need to get a full statement from you tomorrow when you're rested, all right?" To Jack Cassidy he said, "In the meantime, I'm having the Grogans picked up and brought in for questioning." He turned back to Liam. "You were brave," he said sternly, "but you're lucky to be alive."

"No thanks to you," said Delia Cassidy coldly.

Liam shrugged. He was safe. There was nothing more for him to worry about. He could rest. The Mole would pay for his crimes.

The inspector said, "I will order a car to take you home." He gave a stiff little nod to Delia Cassidy and moved off toward the elevator.

Delia Cassidy turned to Liam. "You're shivering, lovey. Are we all finished here?"

"Yes, finished," he said. "It's over."

The Cassidys smiled. Rory looped an arm round Liam's shoulders.

Delia Cassidy said, "Then let's go home."

...a wedding picture...

When they got outside they ran through a heavy shower to the waiting police car.

The police car soon had them home.

They hurried through into the warm kitchen. Delia Cassidy plugged in the kettle. "A drop of tea will warm us up."

Liam stood and looked out the now-repaired kitchen window—the one that had been shattered by the Mole's bullet. He watched a starling picking about in the patch of grass near the garbage can in the tiny backyard. The rain had stopped. A shaft of bright sun cut through the clouds and lit the bird and the patch of grass. He listened to the whistle of the teakettle and the sound of Jack Cassidy humming under his breath as he rinsed cups and saucers in the sink.

He was safe here.

He slept.

The next morning, Delia Cassidy handed him a gold ring. He looked at it in the palm of his hand. She said, "It was your mother's marriage band. Now it's yours. And this too." She handed him a chrome pocket watch on a silver-colored chain. He knew it well. He released the catch, looked at the fine black roman numerals on the white watch face, closed the front again, and weighed the watch in his hand, remembering the frown that creased his da's forehead whenever he squinted to read the time. This was Liam's inheritance: a wedding ring and a watch. His throat filled up. He pushed the ring onto the middle finger of his left hand and dropped the watch into his pocket.

"And here." She held out the key to his house across the street. "You might want to pick up some of your things before the landlord empties the place."

He made no move to take the key. He didn't want to cross the street and go inside the house where his mum and his da had been murdered.

"You do not have to go, of course, if you don't want to."

There were things he would like to keep, things that belonged to his mum and his da, but…

Delia Cassidy read his mind. "Will I come with you?"

"No, that's okay." He took the key from her hand. "I'll go alone."

He crossed the street. It felt strange going in. The house looked the same but felt different. Empty. Damaged. Defiled. He hated it now.

The smashed front door was gone. A second-hand one hung in its place. Probably from the builder's demolition yard. It was a brick color that did not match the dark green trim round the windows. Not that it mattered. The whole street was a mixture of mismatched colors, including the curbs outside the houses, painted the colors of the Irish Republic: green, white, and orange (or gold), meant to symbolize peace (white) between the Irish Republic (green) and the Protestant North (orange). Some white peace, thought Liam. Red would be more like it.

It wasn't the new door so much as the inside of the house itself that gave him the tight feeling in his chest, like his heart was being squeezed and he couldn't breathe.

He climbed the stairs. The door to his mum and da's room was closed.

Frightened at what he might see, he stood outside the door, steeling himself to enter. He didn't have to go in, he knew that; he could simply pass it by. But he gritted his teeth and opened the door and stood staring in. He could see the mess the bullets had made of the walls and the floor. The bed was gone. The rest of the furniture was shattered. Someone, probably the women on the street, had scrubbed and tidied the room. There was no blood that he could see. One step forward and he was inside the room, heart thumping. He saw a picture frame lying face down on the wrecked chest of drawers. He picked it up. It was a wedding picture: his mum and da when they got married, just the two of them, photographed cheek-to-cheek, smiling and happy, posing for the camera, his da in a suit and tie and his mum in a white dress. Both the picture frame and the glass were broken, but the picture was intact. He stared at it and felt his throat muscles thicken and his eyes fill with tears.

For the first time since their deaths, he let it all out. It was like a dam breaking.

He cried.

He sat on the floor and he cried.

When he was finished crying, he moved across the hallway to his room. It looked much the same as when he had left it. He took down his circus posters and rolled them up together, along with the picture of his mum and da.

Downstairs, he took a last look at everything: bookshelves full of books, photo albums, his da's newspapers and magazines strewn untidily on the coffee table, the sleeping telly, his mum and his da's library books, his mum's big ball of dark blue wool and a pair of knitting needles left on the couch, the blender on the drain board, cups and saucers in the kitchen sink, the silent kettle...

He took the two photo albums of family snapshots with him and he left the house, closing its door for the very last time.

...police line-up...

The seven men wheeled their wheelchairs into a brightly lighted room and lined up against a white wall. Each man wore a number on his chest.

It was a police line-up. Liam watched from a window in a separate room. There were three others with him: Jack Cassidy, Inspector Osborne, and a police assistant.

"The wheelchairs are from the hospital," the inspector explained. "It's got to be a level playing field: each man the same."

It was now November, and Belfast was well into its rainy season. A full four months had gone by since the Mole had toppled off the city hall dome, four months since Liam had been living in his new home with the Cassidy family.

He examined the faces of the men in the line-up. The Mole was the second man from the right, number six. He would know the man anywhere. He still saw him in his nightmares. He felt himself trembling. Jack Cassidy's big hand squeezed his shoulder.

Inspector Osborne spoke quietly to his assistant, seated at a desk in the room, and then turned to Liam. "Look at these men. Take your time. If you see the man who broke into your home and shot your parents, just tell me the number on his chest."

Without hesitation Liam said, "Number six."

"You sure?"

"I'm sure."

Jack Cassidy gave his shoulder another firm squeeze.

Inspector Osborne nodded to his assistant, and the men in the wheelchairs were led out of the room.

"It is all up to the police now," said Jack Cassidy as they left the station. "Everything is in their hands."

"Will they keep him in jail, do you think?"

"Didn't you pick him out? Without hesitation. I watched you. You hardly looked at the others. It was obviously the right man, no question. I'm sure they will keep him in jail."

"I hope they lock him up for ever and ever."

"You were very brave in there, Liam. I was proud of you."

"I didn't feel brave. I thought he would see me and jump out of his wheelchair and kill me."

One evening a short time later, Liam opened the door to Inspector Osborne.

"May I come in?"

Delia Cassidy, working in the kitchen, heard his voice. "Come in out of the rain, Inspector."

Liam stepped back and the inspector entered. "She's in the kitchen. Give me your coat and go on through. There's a fresh pot of tea just made."

The three of them sat at the kitchen table. Delia Cassidy poured three cups of tea. "Jack and Rory are down at Rob O'Brien's, helping him fix his old car," she told the inspector.

Inspector Osborne looked tired. He helped himself to milk and sugar. Liam and Delia Cassidy sat stirring their tea in silence, waiting for him to speak.

"Officer Cameron Bentley—or the Mole as you call him, Liam—will be spending the rest of his life in that wheelchair, the one he had at the line-up." The inspector placed his teaspoon carefully, absently, in the saucer. "And in a couple of months or so, he will be facing two charges of murder—your parents—and one charge of attempted murder—you."

"I pray to God they send him to prison for the rest of his life," said Delia Cassidy.

Inspector Osborne said, "If he's found guilty…"

"Of course the man will be found guilty!" said Delia Cassidy.

"If he's found guilty," repeated the inspector, "a life sentence would be the usual penalty. But the prosecutor plea-bargained the Mole into revealing the name of his accomplice. The Mole will probably serve only fifteen years instead of a life sentence."

"I don't get it," said Liam. "Do you mean the Mole gets a lighter sentence in exchange for ratting on his partner?"

"Yes," said Osborne. "That's right. The name of the Mole's partner-in-crime is Kenny Dill. Dill has masterminded many killings, including those of your parents, but we could never pin anything on him before; he was too clever. Now we have a warrant out for his arrest. We also know now, for sure, that the killing of your parents was a senseless retaliation strike, as we'd suspected." He shrugged. "It could have been anybody. It didn't matter to them."

Liam looked at Delia Cassidy.

She took his hand and held it tight.

As far as Liam was concerned, it was all over. The Mole was in jail and soon, by the sounds of it, the other murderer would be in jail too. "What about Grogan?" he asked the inspector.

"Fergus Grogan will also testify. He will say that Bentley threatened and bribed him into helping catch you. He will probably get a reduced sentence for aiding and abetting. Three to five maybe."

"Years?"

The inspector nodded. "Moira Grogan wasn't in on it, as far as we can tell, so she goes free. She was fired from the security division of course."

When Inspector Osborne had gone, Liam sat down and sipped at a second cup of tea with Delia Cassidy.

"Ah, the man isn't all that bad," she said with a sniff. "For a policeman, that is." She gave another sniff. "It's just happy, I am, that he did his job and you're safe."

They sat in silence for a minute.

"Rory is delighted you're living here with us, did I tell you that?"

He shook his head.

"Jack wanted children. We both did. But we could have only the one. Now Rory has the brother we always wanted for him." She looked at him fondly. "And don't ye look enough alike to be twins?" She laughed, delighted with herself.

That night, when he went to bed, he felt emptied but new. It was as if he were starting over. He had a new family.

Rory, in the next bed, was quiet, leaving him be. Liam was grateful for this. He didn't need a lot of talk, not right now.

Tomorrow was Saturday, and he and Rory would take the bus to the city, to the Youth Circus, and things would be just the way they used to be.

Almost.

He would see Nicole again.

Life would go on.

Appendix

These are a few of the dates that Liam memorized in school:

1170 AD: the king of England declares himself king of Ireland as well, which leads to war. Ireland loses.

1609: England gives Irish land to Protestant settlers from Scotland. Catholics are forbidden to own land, vote, or speak the Irish language. The Irish keep fighting for their freedom.

1829: the Irish people win the right to vote.

1916: a small Irish rebellion in Dublin. England wins once again, and Irish leaders are executed or jailed. Angry Irish patriots join Sinn Fein ("ourselves alone"), a non-violent political group fighting for freedom. Many others join the IRA (Irish Republican Army), led by Michael Collins, to fight with weapons.

1921: Michael Collins forces England to allow self-government and freedom for all parts of Ireland except the mainly Protestant north, now known as Northern Ireland or Ulster, where most Catholics still have no vote and no control.

1968: Catholics in the North of Ireland (who do not use the terms Northern Ireland or Ulster), inspired by Martin Luther King in the United States, start to form civil rights groups, fighting non-violently for equal rights with Protestants. They organize protest marches, forbidden by the government. The protestors are attacked and gassed. Catholic homes, neighborhoods and churches are attacked by Protestant mobs. The Catholics arm themselves and begin to fight back. England sends troops to keep the peace.

1972: Bloody Sunday. Fourteen unarmed Catholic protestors are killed by the British army in the North of Ireland. More patriots join the IRA to fight the British. Fighting grows worse. Many lose their lives in twenty-five years of violence.

NB: Catholics are usually identified as Nationalists or Republicans. Protestants are often identified as Loyalists.

1997: cease fire declared.

1998: April 10 peace accord (Good Friday Agreement) is signed. Catholic rights are guaranteed by government, but violence is still not completely eradicated, e.g. four months later, on August 15, twenty-nine people (and two unborn twin girls) are killed in Omagh; many hundreds are left physically and mentally scarred. March 15, 1999, Rosemary Nelson, solicitor, is killed by a bomb in Lurgan, County Armagh.

NB: The story is set in 1999, but the events in the Ardoyne area described in the narrative are actually more recent. Holy Cross is a girls' school.

James Heneghan is the author of a number of award-winning books for young readers, including *Hit Squad*, an Orca Soundings novel, and *Waiting for Sarah* (Orca). James was born in Liverpool, England and now lives in Vancouver, British Columbia.